ENTANGLEMENT

ALSO BY GREGG BRADEN

BOOKS

Deep Truth
The Divine Matrix
Fractal Time
The God Code
The Isaiah Effect*
Secrets of the Lost Mode of Prayer
The Spontaneous Healing of Belief

CD PROGRAMS

An Ancient Magical Prayer (with Deepak Chopra)
Awakening the Power of a Modern God
Deep Truth (abridged audio book)
The Divine Matrix (abridged audio book)
The Divine Name (with Jonathan Goldman)
Fractal Time (abridged audio book)
The Gregg Braden Audio Collection*
Speaking the Lost Language of God
The Spontaneous Healing of Belief (abridged audio book)
Unleashing the Power of the God Code

*All the above are available from Hay House
except items marked with an asterisk.

Please visit Hay House USA: **www.hayhouse.com**®
Hay House Australia: **www.hayhouse.com.au**
Hay House UK: **www.hayhouse.co.uk**
Hay House South Africa: **www.hayhouse.co.za**
Hay House India: **www.hayhouse.co.in**

ENTANGLEMENT

A *Tales of Everyday Magic* Novel

GREGG BRADEN

and Lynn Lauber

Based on a screenplay by Ellen Lewis
and Michael Goorjian

VISIONS

HAY HOUSE, INC.
Carlsbad, California • New York City
London • Sydney • Johannesburg
Vancouver • Hong Kong • New Delhi

Published and distributed in the United States by: Hay House, Inc.: www.hayhouse.com® • *Published and distributed in Australia by:* Hay House Australia Pty. Ltd.: www.hayhouse .com.au • *Published and distributed in the United Kingdom by:* Hay House UK, Ltd.: www.hayhouse.co.uk • *Published and distributed in the Republic of South Africa by:* Hay House SA (Pty), Ltd.: www.hayhouse.co.za • *Distributed in Canada by:* Raincoast: www.raincoast.com • *Published in India by:* Hay House Publishers India: www.hayhouse.co.in

Cover design: Mario San Miguel • *Interior design:* Julie Davison

The authors of this book do not dispense medical advice or prescribe the use of any technique as a form of treatment for physical, emotional, or medical problems without the advice of a physician, either directly or indirectly. The intent of the authors is only to offer information of a general nature to help you in your quest for emotional and spiritual well-being. In the event you use any of the information in this book for yourself, which is your constitutional right, the authors and the publisher assume no responsibility for your actions.

This is a work of fiction. Names, characters, places, and incidents are the product of the authors' imagination or are used fictitiously. Any resemblance to actual events or locales, or persons living or deceased, is strictly coincidental.

Library of Congress Control Number: 2012937084

Tradepaper ISBN: 978-1-4019-3783-6
Digital ISBN: 978-1-4019-3784-3

15 14 13 12   4 3 2 1
1st edition, June 2012

Printed in the United States of America

*"Science cannot
solve the ultimate
mystery of nature.
And that is because,
in the last analysis,
we ourselves are a part
of the mystery . . ."*

— MAX PLANCK

Whistling, a janitor wielded an old-fashioned string mop in front of him as he worked his way down a silent high school hallway. He was slender and in his 60s, grateful to have a steady job, unlike so many others in his family. He came from western Jamaica, where work was scarce. As he worked, he daydreamed about the mists of the Blue Mountains near where he was born.

Out the windows bloomed another San Francisco April—cloudless, mild, the trees a tender green. The janitor passed the administrative offices, busy with the soft clicking of computer keyboards, then the empty lobby—a long, silent stretch of glass cases. These were filled with trophies from the school's students that had accumulated over the 50 years of its existence; basketball and football awards were the most common.

The rest of the cases held photographs of students and faculty now gone. They began with the bright Kodachromes of the early '60s—yellow-haired cheerleaders with pink lips and red outfits—and ended with digital photos, printed on streaked paper. Along the way, every style of the last half century seemed to be represented—country western, hippie, punk rock, goth, and every variant in between.

Several faces stood out from the hundreds showcased. One female graduate from 1969 had an Afro so massive that it exceeded the photograph's frame. A blond boy from the '70s was a dead ringer for John Denver, with a moptop haircut and granny glasses. A more recent photo was of a fresh-faced boy with high cheekbones, a pierced nose, and a face both handsome and sensitive, his flowing tresses tucked behind his ears. Beside this was a photo with the same face, unpierced, with shorter hair and a more intense expression. These images had stopped many visitors who did double takes of these young men—the only identical twins in the 2005 graduating class.

As the janitor moved on, he passed by the science classrooms on the first floor. In the first, Mr. Hadley, a dinosaur of a teacher with thick black-framed glasses and a droning voice, was putting another class to sleep with his explanation of the Pleistocene epoch. Most of the students had their heads down on their desks; others sent texts from their laps.

ENTANGLEMENT

In the next room, a new teacher in her 20s, prim and Southern, tried to control a class of boisterous older students as she discussed the intricacies of cross-pollination. A diagram of a stamen and pistil were on the front board, but no one was paying attention. Several students near the doorway were occupied with fast-food breakfasts; one poured syrup over a stack of pancakes in a Styrofoam container. Cell phones buzzed and beeped.

The last classroom in the hallway was different; it seemed to be stopped in time. A Bunsen burner flamed in a corner. A diagram of an atom hung on the wall; a chart of the solar system covered the ceiling. The chalkboard was covered with a long, complex formula. The only items that revealed the current era were a row of personal computers lined up against the wall, but no one was using them today.

Instead a dozen students of various shapes and sizes were listening raptly to their teacher, Peter Keller. At 42, his salt-and-pepper hair was tousled, his eyes were a light blue-green, and his white dress shirt was rolled up at the sleeves. There was a rumpled, weary look to his face that did not diminish his vitality. He seemed lit by some passionate inner glow, as he held forth with the grace and nimbleness of an actor.

Keller's students listened to him intently as he measured two ounces of water and poured them into an empty soda can. Using tongs, he carefully lowered the can into place over a heated Bunsen burner. Year after year, his introductory physics class was the school's most popular, often with a waiting list in case someone dropped out, though that rarely happened. He had a reputation for kindling in students a new respect for and interest in science. Perhaps because of this, many of them developed long-term secret crushes on him, though he barely noticed and never encouraged them. In fact, outside the classroom, Keller was quiet, shy, and somewhat mysterious.

Standing behind a lab table, he now turned to his students.

"Let me ask you a question. Why does a man float when you throw him into the water, but a book sinks?"

A husky boy named Eddie Campos, who sported a blond mohawk and was the class clown, said, "I don't float. I tried swimming once. I'm telling you, I sank like a stone."

The students laughed.

"Mr. Campos, let me put it this way, then: why does everybody except you float, while a book sinks?"

"Density," Eddie answered.

"Thank you. Clearly you're not so dense. So I have no idea why you don't float."

The students chuckled again. There was an intimate, congenial feeling in the classroom.

Eddie asked, "Isn't density also why fancy drinks with layers work?"

"Yes. But unfortunately, fancy drinks with layers won't be on the final. Any other random questions while we wait?"

A slight, green-eyed boy wearing a hooded sweatshirt raised his hand.

"Yes, Colin?"

"When do we get to quantum physics?"

"After we finish with standard physics . . . which, at the rate we're going, should be sometime around 2017."

"I hear that quantum physics makes time travel possible. I'd be into that."

Peter smiled. "Right, so did you want to go to the future or the past?"

"I think the past—when things were more simple."

"Really?" Keller said. "So you'd like to read by candlelight; warm yourself by a fire, assuming you had enough wood or coal; and travel by foot or horse, so you'd essentially remain in the same area all your life. Oh, also hunt for your own food—in other words, shoot it or fish for it—or go hungry. You're pining for that?"

Colin smiled sheepishly and shook his head. "Not when you put it that way."

"Well, that, my friend, isn't the way *I'd* put it; that's the way life has been in most places until the last hundred years or so, and some places even now." The teacher looked out the window for a moment, in contemplation. "Actually, Einstein's theories do suggest that time travel is possible;

however, there are a few glitches to work out, so not anytime soon. Next question?"

Colin continued, "But isn't it true that there's so much space inside an atom that we should be able to walk through walls?"

"Theoretically, yes. But the probability is so absurdly infinitesimal that you'd have to try for an extremely long time. You're welcome to give it a shot. There's a wall right back there, Mr. Morley."

Peter gestured to a wall at the back of the room, inviting Colin to try.

Colin smiled and shook his head.

Monica Bennett, a nervous, soft-voiced brunette, raised her hand. Mr. Keller pointed to her.

"What happened before the Big Bang?"

The alpha girl in class—the tall, angular, dark-haired Jane Sinclair—snickered. "That's a stupid question," she scoffed.

Keller gave her a narrow look. "Is it a question you know the answer to, Ms. Sinclair?"

"Well . . ." She blushed to the roots of her hair and lowered her eyes, indicating that she didn't.

"Well, neither do I," Keller said. "If anyone figures it out, they win the Nobel Prize, and the winner has to take me to Stockholm."

John Segal, a jock with an impish face, leaned back in his chair.

"My older brother had you, and he said that you used to work for the government building bombs or something. Is that true?"

"Who's your brother?"

"David Segal."

"*The* David Segal who got caught smoking pot behind the portables?"

"Uh, yeah."

There was general laughter.

"I think your brother confused the building of bongs with the building of bombs, somehow," Peter mused, widening his eyes for effect. The students chuckled.

"Next question."

Monica Bennett raised her hand.

"Yes?" Peter asked.

"I think the water's boiling."

Peter looked at the soda can. "So it is. Okay! Everybody put on your goggles and gather round."

The students put on their goggles and moved forward until they were in a circle around Peter, who pulled on his own goggles.

"Where's the bucket?"

Colin got a white plastic bucket filled with cold water. He set it on the floor beside the lab table.

"Everybody ready?" Peter asked. "Eddie, where are your goggles?"

Eddie Campos found them and pulled them on.

"Okay," Keller said. "What do you think's going to happen?"

Campos said, "Water's gonna squirt all over us."

Peter looked around. "Anyone else?"

"The tab'll pop off, and hot water will come out," Colin ventured.

Josh Segal said, "I don't think anything will happen."

Peter said, "Okay, let's see." He carefully removed the soda can from over the Bunsen burner with a pair of tongs, then in one swift, sure motion turned it over and plunged it into the bucket of cold water—where it collapsed. A wave of approval swept over the class.

"That was awesome," Eddie Campos said. "Good one, Mr. Keller."

The bell rang, and the students bolted for their chairs, grabbed their books and bags, and yanked off their goggles. Peter turned off the Bunsen burner and pulled off his goggles as well.

"On Monday, I want a paper from each of you on the physics behind the collapsing soda can!"

As the students scrambled for the exit, Peter glanced out the window; a heavy rain had started falling. Then he crossed to the front of the room, where a large projection screen hung down in front of the chalkboard. He stared at the screen with a contemplative expression as the last student left the room.

The door closed and Peter was alone. He rubbed his eyes, then turned to a filing cabinet at the side of his desk and, using a key, unlocked it. He dug inside, searching, and in the process pulled out a black-and-white photo—a beautiful young woman, olive-skinned, her almond-shaped eyes peering into the camera. He retrieved a book and a meditation pillow.

He placed the photo on top of a large stack of papers on his desk, then leafed through the book. Finally he turned to the projection screen at the front of the room and began to raise it.

"Peter?"

Startled, he quickly pulled the screen back down again, covering what was on the chalkboard. Standing in the open door was Dori Morgan, the school's honors French teacher. Blonde and gray-eyed, with a warm smile and gentle laugh, Dori had asked him out for coffee several times, but he'd never followed up.

"Hey, Peter. I was curious, are you attending the district board meeting tonight?" she asked. "Maybe we could drive together."

Peter fiddled with some papers and turned away. "Mmm, no. I've got so much grading to do."

Dori laughed. "It's Friday, Peter."

She leaned against the door frame expectantly. He could smell her perfume. The scientist in him tried to break it down: it smelled like equal parts citrus oil and something else, maybe jasmine.

She was getting too near—for a number of reasons. Peter was afraid that she'd see a paper of hers that he'd promised to edit months ago that was now part of the large neglected pile on his desk, including much of his own work that he simply had to gather and submit to various journals. Somehow, he hadn't been able to muster the effort. The pile also included several more photos of the same woman. Manuela. Peter moved his body slightly in an effort to shield all of this from Dori's gaze.

"Sorry I haven't looked at your paper yet," he said. A preemptive strike was best, he decided.

"Oh, that's okay. No worries." She smiled good-naturedly. "Are you sure you don't want to come?"

"Next time," he said.

"Well, I don't want to bother you." She turned to leave, but hesitated, giving him a chance to change his mind. "Have a good weekend."

"You, too," he said without looking up, moving papers around on his desk.

"See you Monday, then."

"Monday. Definitely. Enjoy that meeting," he replied.

He turned and watched her walk away with feelings so mixed that he couldn't begin to sort them out.

With her thick flaxen hair and beautifully placid face, she was as attractive as the Swedish film stars he'd loved as a youth. Given time, he'd hoped that some bond would develop between them, but it hadn't happened yet.

In many ways, they were perfectly suited for each other. She was divorced and without children. Her life was centered on school, where she worked the same long hours he did. They were close in age, unlike some of the women Peter had met, who'd never even heard of Motown.

Dori listened to him talk with a grave and evident interest. There was even a spark between them when they brushed hands. But he stomped out any feeling. It made him feel guilty.

The last time he'd talked to her was when she'd left the paper that he'd placed on the pile with all the other things he meant to do—manuscripts he wanted to publish, photos he meant to sort through and frame, or put in albums. And there it sat still.

This all had to do with the woman in the photo. Manuela.

CHAPTER 2

Peter had met Manuela when he worked at Fermilab, one of the country's leading research laboratories. He'd just graduated from MIT, approaching the height of his scientific career, well on his way to becoming a star.

She was the only woman he'd ever been involved with who hadn't been overly impressed by him, who hadn't put him on a pedestal. Only once, when he'd talked to her about a theory called *quantum entanglement,* had she seem intrigued.

"Quantum entanglement suggests that once particles are connected, they remain connected on an energetic level, even when they are physically separated from one another. And the really interesting thing is that whether the separation is only a few millimeters or an entire galaxy, the distance doesn't appear to affect the connection. Quantum entanglement exists in the real world, but we can't see it. We can feel it, however, once that filament of connection is forged."

"Entanglement, yes," she said and wrapped her arms around him. "That is what this is." She held him so close that he could feel the heat of her body and take in the scent of her long black hair, so sweetly aromatic, as if she had recently immersed herself in the essence of tropical flowers. They were in bed, where they'd spent many hours during the first period of their romance. She made him feel like a besotted schoolboy, not a highly respected scientist.

She was from Guatemala—her mother was a housekeeper who'd brought her over when she was 16 from the village of Santiago Atitlán to study. Manuela was working her way through college while buffing floors, and ended up on the cleaning staff at Fermilab while Peter was there. With her dark hair and Mayan face, she stood out amid all the beige, milky blondes he had known in the past.

Before they started dating, he'd observed her on more than one occasion hovering near his office door, listening in as he discussed the progress of his work. The first time they talked, he'd sat down beside her in the crowded cafeteria after he had seen her loitering again near his door. She sat alone, looking mysterious and inscrutable . . . she ate from a fragrant, somewhat greasy bag that her mother had packed for her.

"I noticed you were listening in on my presentation," Peter said to her, diving into his burger and fries.

"Yes," she answered. "Your class is very popular. Do you like cheese enchiladas?"

He was stunned. No fawning; no bullshit. An immediate sense of intimacy between them. This, he would learn, was her way.

"Yes," he answered, and she handed over two warm envelopes of melted cheese and spices that were among the best things he'd ever tasted in his life.

After that, they ate beside each other often, sometimes barely speaking. But Manuela's presence was powerful. Even when she was absent, Peter felt her at his side.

Finally he asked her if she wanted to go out for a movie or dinner—activities that he thought were probably too conventional to suit her, and he'd been right.

"No movie, but I will take a stroll with you or cook for you, whatever you prefer," she said as she presented her splendid white smile.

It turned out that she possessed her own private genius; she knew trees by both their leaves and bark, birds by their songs and feathers. If you wanted to discern the patterns of stars or to identify a butterfly, she was the one to ask. Peter had never encountered anyone like her.

Soon they were having dinner at her house almost every week, and afterward they took long walks, not returning until it was nearly dark. For a long time before he advanced to kissing her, she only let him hold her hand, and then eventually she let him stay the night in her tiny studio apartment. He fell in love with her with so little fanfare that he barely noticed it happening. Still, he had begun fantasizing a future with her; he imagined marrying her and living in a secluded farmhouse with their acutely beautiful daughters.

Man proposes, God disposes. Whoever said that was a genius.

Instead, Peter had continued with his life as before: working all hours on his research. He—and everyone else who worked at the lab—felt sure he was on the brink of a great new discovery. Some days he was so embroiled in his job that he neglected to return Manuela's calls.

He would make it up to her, he told himself; yet later, he couldn't remember if he'd ever told her how much he loved her.

CHAPTER 3

Across town on a side street stood a white brick warehouse with "100" written in blue masking tape on the side. During the neighborhood's heyday, milk bottles in thick glass and unusual shapes had been manufactured inside that building. For decades after the company went under, it had stood vacant, until a local businessman bought it for student apartments. Now it was carved into cavernous living spaces and art studios—a sanctuary for the town's bohemians, artists, and musicians.

The driving beat of tribal/techno music blended with rain beating down on the rambling old building. As usual, a raging party was going this weekend.

The large open space was divided by curtains and occupied by different factions. A group of young men practiced a fire performance, spinning poles, chains, and other objects; another group sat huddled together discussing world affairs. Bits and pieces of conversation could be heard in the din.

"A couple of people, like in Egypt, they make it look like a bad thing," a young man with elaborate facial piercings was saying.

"Is it all programming, or is there something to the energy of the actual location?"

In another section, filled with plants, trees, and indoor fountains, a girl with long braids, Alma, stood reading poetry aloud to a circle of friends, turning it into a performance piece with sudden moments of dancing. And under a parachute canopy, another group of kids drank, smoked, and waxed philosophical, debating chakras and alien abduction.

Wedged between two people on a secondhand couch sat Jack Franklin. Long-haired, pierced, and lean, his upper body extensively tattooed, he sat listening. His face usually had an open, contemplative quality, but tonight he looked troubled and preoccupied. He took a swig when a vodka bottle was passed around; the rest of the crowd was guzzling from the same bottle and passing a joint. Jack held the joint in his fingers for a moment, then passed it on. He rubbed his temples and shut his eyes. He was having trouble following the thread of conversation. Finally, he stood up to leave.

His friend, a gaunt blond with a shaved head named Sam, broke off from his conversation when he saw Jack leaving, and followed.

"What's up, man? You seem out of it tonight."

"Yeah, I can't concentrate. My head's killing me. I don't know what it is."

Sam looked at him with concern.

"You've seemed off all night."

"Just tired. I'll catch you later."

Sam, the son of one of the town's wealthier families, claimed to be a socialist. He lived on a few hundred a month from his trust fund and gave the rest away to whatever charity moved him at the moment.

Jack found his friend's attitude both noble and unnerving. As someone who often didn't have enough money to make it through the week, watching Sam try to decide what he should do with his extra cash each month was often more than he could bear.

Especially since the warehouse was in constant need of repair. The landlord lived in another state and was deaf to complaints about termites, leaks, and faulty plumbing. Usually the residents simply waited until someone happened along with the requisite skills to fix whatever was broken.

"You can give some money to me, man," Jack said on several occasions, and though Sam was agreeable, Jack found that he was unable to accept it in the end.

As he walked away now, he rubbed his eyes as if to clear his vision. For a moment, he leaned against the wall in dizziness and disorientation. Again he touched his temple and took a few deep breaths. What was wrong with him?

Alma rushed up and put her arm around him. "Hey, sweetie, you okay?"

With her long, braided hair and large eyes, Alma had an innocent, almost childlike demeanor that Jack found alluring. They had lived together, off and on, in his small room, but at the moment they had rooms of their own. Alma wore a pearl ring he'd bought for her during a euphoric early weekend that they'd spent together traveling the coast. She wore it on her ring finger; it was unclear what she believed it symbolized. Jack had thought only that the ring was pretty and had wanted to buy her a gift. He cared for Alma, but had yet to have the experience of wanting to spend his life with one woman. He'd never had the heart to tell her this, however.

They stood in a tight hallway, her fingers interlaced with his. He stood against the brick wall, and she kissed his cheek.

"What's wrong? You don't seem like yourself," she whispered.

Jack buried his face in her hair but pulled away as she began kissing his neck. His eyes were closed, and he was unresponsive.

"Not in the mood?"

Jack wrapped his arms around her waist. "It doesn't have anything to do with you."

Alma pulled back and looked closely at his face. "Who does it have to do with?"

"I just need to be alone right now. I'm having a rough time."

Alma blanched. "I've never heard you say *that* before."

"I've never *felt* like this before," Jack said. "It's about my brother—I'll tell you about it later."

Alma still looked almost tearful. Seeing her face, he gathered her closer to him. "Everything's cool with us. It'll be okay."

"You sure?"

Jack kissed her lightly. "Yes, I'm sure. I'll see you later."

He headed toward his room and parted the batik curtain that served as his door. Inside was a mattress, a video-editing dock, a computer, and a pile of clothes. He pulled off his shirt, kicked off his combat boots, and threw himself down on the mattress, putting his hand on his head.

Jack had lived in this room for almost two years, ever since he and Charlie, his twin brother, had gone their separate ways. A part-time art student, Jack had received a short-term scholarship that had recently ended. Now, in order to make ends meet, he had to work three different odd jobs and share a floor of the warehouse with a group of friends.

Decorating the walls were photocopies of his digital creations—vines, tentacles, and futuristic landscapes, somewhere between cyber and organic. Beside the bed was a stack of books by a variety of authors, philosophers, and theorists: Albert Camus, Buckminster Fuller, Khalil Gibran, Aldous Huxley.

He grabbed one from the top of the stack and tried to read, but he couldn't concentrate. He finally tossed the book down and turned off the light.

The ceiling above his bed was decorated with glow-in-the-dark stickers of the solar system—hundreds of stars, moons, and planets.

Jack stared at the sky above him, his breathing heavy. Something was very wrong. His chest felt constricted, as if something were sitting on it. As he shut his eyes, he was overcome by a dreamlike vision, a series of disjointed images, all set in the desert. There were hands on a Humvee steering wheel, a flash of a khaki uniform, the sound of an engine grinding its gears.

Sunglasses reflected the white-hot sun and miles of desert. The sweating face of his twin brother, Charlie, suddenly looked up at a hilltop ridge to the left of the Humvee, where there stood a strange creature. A coyote or a wolf? Then, a male scream, a sudden flash of light, and a loud ringing in his ears.

Jack jumped up, covered in sweat. "Charlie!" he cried, just as the coyote's face also appeared at the foot of his bed with a great snarl. Jack was breathing fast, his eyes wild as he looked around.

"Oh, God—oh, God!"

He stood up and rooted around frantically in the clothes on the floor until he found his cell phone. He flipped it open and pushed buttons until he came to his senses. Charlie was in Afghanistan. He couldn't be reached on a cell phone.

He moved over to his desk. The screen on his laptop lit up, reflecting his own panicked face. When he tried to get online, a message popped up as he opened the browser: "No connection available." He tried to log on to Skype, but still the same message appeared. He looked out the window to see a crack of lightning flash across the sky, followed by a low roar of thunder.

"Come on, come on."

He reached down and checked whether the ethernet cable was plugged in and saw that it was. He checked the screen again; still no service. He pounded on his keyboard.

He followed the ethernet cable out of his room, down the hallway, to a high ledge where it ended. Climbing onto the ledge, Jack found that the modem was blinking red.

"Damn it!"

Shirtless, he moved into the large open space where Alma was sitting with a few of her friends on the floor.

"How long's the Internet been down?" he asked her.

"Hi, sweetie! How're you feeling?"

"Why's the Internet down?" he asked.

"I don't know. What's going on?"

He stormed past her into an alcove where Sam sat reading.

Sam gazed at his friend's face. "Dude, what's the matter?"

Jack said, "I need to talk to my brother, and the Internet's down."

"So can't you call him?"

Jack gave him a withering look. "He's in the service—in Afghanistan. How many times have I mentioned that?"

Sam's face turned red. "Sorry, I forgot. But in my defense, you don't actually bring it up much."

"Whatever," Jack said, annoyed. "Can you think of what might be wrong with it?"

Sam shrugged as he stood up. "Maybe Martin didn't pay the bill on time. We'll fix it in the morning, if you can just chill out."

"I can't just chill out," Jack said. "Don't you get it?"

Sam shrugged again. "It's no big deal."

Jack shoved him against the wall. "Don't say it's no big deal. This is my *brother* we're talking about. And the morning's too late—I have to talk to him now."

"Whatever, man. Back off."

Jack removed his hands and stomped to his room again, grabbing a shirt as he dug around for his keys. Then he stuffed his laptop in a messenger bag and headed out into the rainy night.

His Camaro was parked haphazardly on the street, unlocked. He jumped in, turned on the lights, and screeched off.

Or *tried* to screech off. Two blocks later, Jack was stopped by a traffic jam that snaked ahead for what looked like miles. He turned on the radio and heard that a tractor trailer had gotten stuck in the overpass ahead and would remain there until it could be dislodged with special equipment. This happened every few months, and there was no recourse but to shut down his engine and wait it out; it would be at least 20 minutes.

California traffic—he thought as he opened the window and rubbed his eyes. Not that he remembered any other kind. Or did he?

He closed his eyes, and he was back in Ohio. At six years old, he and Charlie sat at the house of their maternal grandmother, Nelly, playing with Legos on the living room floor. It was a late summer day, dry and airless; a rotating fan sat on the floral rug throwing a lazy arc of air.

Jack and Charlie were born on a hot summer night in late July, Jack a few minutes before his brother. Their mother had been hugely pregnant for so long that people had begun thinking she might have triplets. But it had only been the two of them—who, at seven pounds each, had caused her a protracted, difficult labor.

People were forever getting the two of them mixed up, which alternately irked and amused them. Just like in the movies, they played jokes on teachers and girlfriends, who mistook one of them for the other. Even Nelly had to study them long and hard, especially as they emerged from swimming or the shower, when they looked particularly alike.

The boys received nearly the same grades, even when they took a class with a different teacher. They chose the same color and style of clothing from separate catalogs when their mother asked them what they wanted for Christmas. They gravitated toward the same kind of friends—who were loyal and smart—and loved spicy Mexican food, which was difficult to locate in their part of Ohio.

What they shared was endless, so vast and deep that it could not be measured. They both found it comforting to be so close to one another, to feel as if they had a true and constant second self who mirrored them. Who else had that?

They were the only offspring of parents who had once been considered the most successful and good-looking of couples—their mother an intense, high-strung professor with a sharp wit; their father a handsome, towheaded bass player and perpetual hippie. It was commonly said, especially by their grandmother, that the boys had inherited the best qualities of both sides—that they'd combined their mother's brains and competitiveness with their father's cool good looks and effortless charm. They were born in the late '80s, into otherwise childless families, and so were the recipients of double doses of love. But this adoration wasn't enough to keep their parents together for long. Their mother was too cool and aloof, according to their father, while their mother claimed that he was too immature, with an incessantly wandering eye.

The constant in the boys' lives was their grandmother. Nelly often babysat for them and taught them how to play hearts, appreciate country cooking, and sit through Sunday-school lessons, even when they didn't understand the point. She was a longtime widow and remained perpetually thrilled to have them living so close to her—that is, until the afternoon when her daughter announced that they were moving away.

"Elaine, you're not really taking these boys all the way to California?" Nelly asked as they all sat in the living room. She was still wearing the kind of housedress and sensible heels that she'd worn to her job as church secretary every day until her retirement.

Elaine turned on her mother with a look that the boys knew well.

"California is where I found a job, Mother. What else do you want me to do with them? It's the best teaching offer I got anywhere."

"This whole big country, and you're telling me the only place you can find work is fifteen hundred miles away?"

"Yes, that's exactly what I'm saying."

Their grandmother sniffed in disbelief. "And what does Tom say?"

"Tom needs me to work—he's not saying anything. It's not like he's making any money."

Nelly shook her head. "It's no good, I'm telling you. California is no place for these children to grow up."

"And why not? It's warm and beautiful there!"

Before Nelly could answer, the phone rang, and Elaine left to answer it.

The boys looked at each other when their mother was gone, as if conveying some silent message.

Nelly leaned forward. "You listen to me, boys. I want you to remember two things. You ever have any trouble or need anything, you call me collect; I don't care what time."

"What do you mean, *trouble*?" Jack asked.

"You've never lived out west; it's different there. People do whatever they want. Anything goes. It's not like Ohio."

The boys took this in silently.

"And another thing I want you to remember: education. It's what will save you. Make sure you keep on studying, that you go to college. When I'm gone, there'll be money to help you out."

"You act like we're not ever going to see you again," Charlie said.

"Well, you never know. But you won't be living near me anymore, and letters and phone calls are different."

Their father walked into the room, and they immediately fell silent. With his long, pale hair, jeans, and laconic, laid-back manner, he hardly seemed fatherly—he was simply the musician he claimed to be.

"What's happening?" he asked.

"We're talking about California," Nelly told him.

Tom rolled his eyes. "I'm not looking forward to that move. I'm not even sure I can make it. The band's auditioning for a gig . . ."

Elaine reentered and stood with her hands on her hips. "What are you talking about? I haven't heard a word about this."

"Well, it just happened." He lit a cigarette. "We got a call about playing a couple of concerts outside of Pittsburgh. We've been trying to get in there for years now, and we finally got a break. You don't hit it big overnight with my kind of work."

Elaine rolled her eyes.

"What? You're saying I'll never make it, aren't you?"

She raised her hands, palms out. "I didn't say a word."

Listening to their parents, the boys began disassembling their Lego constructions. They had been building a fort, with a reinforced wall and a number of sturdy buildings inside. Now they methodically took them apart. Jack didn't know how it was possible to feel sorry for both of his parents at the same time, but he did, and he knew Charlie felt the same. They nearly always felt the same. They were identical twins, after all, formed when a single fertilized egg had split in two—as close as two humans could ever be.

Tom finished his cigarette, then left, slamming out of the front door, getting into his car, and pulling away.

The boys gathered their Legos together in a large pile.

Finally, Jack said, "Dad's not moving with us."

Charlie said, "I know."

Nelly studied them. "Just remember what I said."

The boys put their Legos in the box and then stood and regarded their grandmother, still sitting regally in her big chair.

"Come here," Nelly said. They both shuffled over and wrapped four arms around her.

Into her silky bodice, Jack murmured, "We'll remember," speaking, as he often did, for them both.

Traffic was in fact one of the few things Nelly *hadn't* warned them about when they moved here years ago. Since she had practically raised them while their mother was teaching and their father was on the road, she remained appalled that they were "taken" away from her and their relatively staid life in northwestern Ohio.

The move to San Francisco had heralded the end of their parents' marriage, just as the boys had predicted, but as long as they had each other, they felt certain they'd survive.

Jack stared at the windshield wipers, the rain beating against them. He looked at the clock. He'd been sitting here for 15 minutes. He turned on the radio again and sat through five minutes of sports scores, weather, and finally the traffic rehash. Ten more minutes of delay was the estimate now. *Shit.* He was stuck. He turned off the radio and looked at his face in the rearview mirror. Something about the light and his state of mind . . . he looked like an old man. He looked like his father.

He leaned back in the seat as another scene popped into his mind. It was the fateful day after their grandmother's funeral.

At that point he and Charlie were fresh out of high school, over six feet tall, and wearing suits that they'd outgrown and dark glasses. Even so, they didn't look perfectly identical anymore.

Since graduating, they'd begun to differentiate themselves in small ways. Charlie had started cutting his hair shorter and dressing in preppier clothes, while Jack let his hair grow to his shoulders, wore beaded necklaces, and got tattoos. Jack had received a scholarship that would pay for several semesters of art school, while Charlie was taking his time, deciding where and when he wanted to go to college. They shared the same opinions, politics, and basic tastes, but Jack hung out with the more avant-garde, arty students in town, while Charlie tended to spend more time with people at his gym.

Losing their grandmother had left them both stunned and sad. They'd traveled back and forth from Ohio in two days—with their morose, silent mother, who took the occasion to let them know that over the years, their father had emptied what had been intended as their college fund.

"Why didn't someone stop him?"

"No one realized he was doing it. I never looked at that money. We all had access to it—unfortunately."

Neither of them could quite digest this news coming so soon after the death of Nelly. They couldn't wait to get back to California. On the plane, both slouched in the cramped coach seats; their faces were a study in dual melancholy.

"I can't remember being so bummed," Jack said. "We not only lose Grandma, but now there's no money."

"We'll have to find real work," Charlie said. Both had worked odd jobs—Charlie in construction, Jack stocking grocery shelves.

"Right. We'll be old men before we save up enough. Do you know how much school costs now? Art school will be twenty grand a year once my scholarship's over. And my friend's paying forty thousand a year for a state college."

"We'll do it somehow. We just have to make a plan."

"Let me know when you figure one out."

"I've already got an idea."

Two days later, when Jack walked downstairs and saw that Charlie had invited a recruiter to meet him, he was flabbergasted. He looked at the man's uniform in amazement.

"Who are *you?*"

"He's a marine," Charlie said. "His name's William." He turned slightly. "This is my brother."

"A *marine?*" Jack looked William up and down as if sizing him up for a fight. He was in his late 30s, with a buzz cut, ramrod-straight posture, and a smooth face. He looked like a former football player.

"Nice to meet you, son," William said coolly, extending his hand and quickly placing it in his pocket when Jack didn't move.

"Don't tell me you're considering *enlisting,*" Jack said. "Are you *serious?*"

"Yes, he's serious," William said, as if *he* were Charlie's twin and privy to his deepest thoughts.

"Man, you've got to be kidding."

William winked at Charlie, infuriating Jack even more.

"Jack, it's not the worst thing in the world."

"Oh, really?" Jack ignored William and continued speaking to his brother. "I'm sure he's told you all kinds of great stuff about the adventure and high pay, but wait until you find yourself in the middle of some broiling desert, aiming Patriot missiles at civilians."

William smiled, as if he had heard such false information before. He said, "The Marines are trained, equipped, and organized to maintain a state of constant global readiness. We offer benefits that rival Fortune 500 companies, especially in this kind of economic climate."

"That sounds right out of an advertising brochure," Jack said.

Charlie said to his brother, "Listen, I've been thinking about this for a while. I can get my entire college paid for by joining up—no student loans at all. And with Iraq winding down, there's a good chance I'll end up in the States anyway."

Jack snorted. "Oh, sure. That's what they tell you. But what if they send your ass straight over to Afghanistan? You hate these wars. You're not equipped for fighting and killing people."

Charlie looked away from him. "Speak for yourself, Jack. I know what I'm capable of."

Jack turned his gaze to the recruiter, who seemed to be emanating a smug certitude. Probably Charlie had already signed some contract or other. Weren't they desperate for smart soldiers? And Charlie would be among the smartest and fittest. Jack felt a surge of possessiveness as he looked again at his twin. How could this stranger take him away?

"Did you think I would sign up, too? Is that why you brought him here?"

Charlie smiled. "I didn't think so. But William said that, being twins and all, it'd be kind of cool if we enlisted together."

"Yeah, real cool . . . they could ship us home together in the same box." Jack ran his hands through his hair. He couldn't believe this was happening. "Did you tell Mom yet?"

"Yeah. She freaked out, as you can imagine. Said she couldn't bear to lose me. That we were all she had. Etcetera. She pulled out every stop. I ended up comforting her, and I'm the one who's leaving."

"Can't you take some time to think this over? I mean, this *is* your life we're talking about."

But even as Jack said this, he saw it was too late. Whatever the recruiter had promised, it must have been very beguiling. Charlie was lost.

Jack couldn't help blaming his father for this disaster. If he'd kept his mitts off the money their grandmother had set aside for them, none of this would have happened.

Jack said to the recruiter, "Can my brother and I talk alone for a few minutes?"

William walked down the hall and got on his cell phone.

"You're too smart to do this, bro."

"Jack, I'm not going to walk around owing a hundred-thousand-dollar college loan for the rest of my life."

"I'm not going to do that either."

"You don't have any other *choice*—you'll be in debt if you finish art school. You just told me that tuition's twenty grand. Where will you ever get that?"

"So we'll learn a trade or something. Remember how Grandma always told us that being an electrician or plumber was honorable work? And the pay is good."

Charlie looked at his brother's long hair, pierced ear, and elaborate sleeves of tattoos. "I just can't see you doing that. There are long hours of apprenticeship; you have to get into a union—it's hard work."

"What, you're saying I'm lazy?"

"No, but you're artistic—you've always been more artistic than I am. That's what you're suited for. Doing something with video or computers."

"You always liked that stuff, too."

"Not as much as you. We *do* have differences."

Jack turned away. He didn't like it when Charlie reminded him of this.

That was the last time Jack had seen him face-to-face, in what he considered the Before Time—before the war. Charlie was gone within the week, departing for a base in San Diego for boot camp. Jack looked up the basic training program and saw that, within 21 days, Charlie would have to be able to do 3 pull-ups and 40 sit-ups in 2 minutes, and run 3 miles in 28 minutes. This seemed laughingly impossible, at least to him, and yet Charlie didn't change his mind, as Jack had privately hoped and prayed.

"You didn't even say good-bye," he said when Charlie eventually called him from San Diego.

"They didn't give me much time to get ready. I called, but you weren't there."

And you didn't leave a message? Jack thought but didn't say.

These were new times, separate times. He would not have the access to his twin that he'd always known and mostly taken for granted.

When they hung up, Jack checked his incoming cell calls and saw that Charlie had indeed tried to call him, not once, but nine times, on a day when Jack's cell had been dead in his jacket pocket. At least this made him feel better. Because, otherwise, Charlie was gone, gone, as far away as he'd ever been.

He came home after training for one short and exasperating visit, when he seemed like an automaton, his head shaved, his eyes cool and as if they contained points of steel. Then he was swiftly deployed to Afghanistan, just as Jack had feared.

But this time Charlie made sure he actually spoke to his brother before he left.

"I told you, man—I knew that's where they'd send you," Jack said.

Charlie was silent for a minute. "I thought so, too."

"You did?"

"Yeah. I didn't want a desk job in the States. If I'm doing this, I want to really do it."

Jack still found it amazing that his brother would willingly leave home and engage in becoming a soldier—something so antithetical to what he thought they both believed.

Since Charlie was going to be stationed so far away, Jack began studying possible regions where he might be deployed. The Internet wasn't enough now.

He traveled downtown to the ancient brick library and dragged down volumes of maps and spread them out before him. His brother was in Asia, another continent, even farther away than Africa, near the Red Sea, which Jack vaguely remembered from the Bible. He read aloud the exotic and foreign place names: the Tropic of Cancer, Turkmenistan, the Dardanelles Strait. On the map, the pink-colored Islamic Republic of Afghanistan itself looked unreal, like a puzzle piece. He read how the population was mostly Pashtun; how the average citizen made the equivalent of $1,000 a year; that Kabul, the capital, was also the largest city; and that there were ongoing threats to assassinate U.S. citizens. He could imagine the risk to marines. The time difference between Kabul and San Francisco was 12.5 hours, with San Francisco behind. His brother might as well be on the moon; Jack would have preferred it.

Driving home, he found a brochure that William the recruiter had left behind that had been underlined and annotated in what he realized was Charlie's hand. He read the first paragraph:

"The Middle East is in the vanguard of the War on Terror, and the Marines support this effort with a number of operations. Those deployed in the region regularly provide security services or go into combat, but they may also work as instructors, trainers, protectors, and mentors. In Afghanistan, troops are involved in mentoring and training the country's national army. They may also be involved in combat with insurgent forces."

Charlie had underlined the words *instructors, trainers, protectors,* and *mentors. That's me,* he wrote. But Jack focused on the word *combat.*

Each morning he studied the casualty list in the newspaper with his heart in his throat. Yet even as he exhaled with relief after scanning the list of names, he knew that for someone, somewhere, a name on this list would become the heartache of a lifetime, signifying the loss of a precious someone—father or daughter, son or wife—who could never be replaced.

CHAPTER 4

Charlie sat on patrol duty at five o'clock on a broiling Saturday evening, the sun still beating down on his back like a white-hot hand. He was cradling a heavy, futuristic rifle that had radio-controlled "smart" bullets designed to explode on contact with targets far out of conventional range. There weren't enough of these to go around, and all the soldiers wanted one, but Charlie was half afraid to use it, anxious that it might go off in his face. He was also smoking a cigarette—a habit that he'd picked up within days of deployment.

After basic training, he'd been transported to Wardak province, near Kabul—one of the most dangerous regions in the country. Rumor had it that this was where most newcomers were sent, after the area had taken its toll on more seasoned veterans. Lately there'd been an increase in convoys being ambushed and government officials being killed.

Charlie had witnessed one weary platoon pulling out as his moved in. He'd never beheld such grizzled faces on young men before. Sunburned, their beards sprinkled with what looked like salt, their eyes beyond weary.

"That'll be us," said his new friend Ernesto, smoking beside him.

"We'll be lucky if that *is* us."

"What do you mean?"

The answer was so obvious that he didn't bother to say it.

Ernesto was the kind of friend he probably wouldn't have had back in the States. Hispanic, a staunch Catholic, and already a father of two at 25, Ernesto worked at a chicken plant in southern Missouri and was the most important person in Charlie's immediate world. Ernesto already knew the ropes, so he kept an eye on Charlie as they scrambled up the mountainous terrain together. His new friend had even given Charlie a Saint Christopher medal. Charlie didn't know what it signified exactly, but he was grateful for it and wore it always.

At night, on patrols like this one, Ernesto talked about his family, especially his wife.

"I don't know if she'll wait for me if I'm gone much longer," he told Charlie, who was shocked, though he tried to hide it.

"But why not? And what about the kids?"

"She's hot, man. You saw her picture. She could find someone else to look after the kids. She probably don't think I'll be making it back anyhow."

Charlie contemplated this as Ernesto studied him. "What about you? Don't you have a girl?"

"Yeah, her name's Hannah. I don't know how she's feeling about me right now. We had a big fight about my enlisting."

"She didn't want you to go?"

"Nope. Basically she found my papers before I told her, and she took it like a betrayal or something."

Ernesto shook his head.

"And my mother was just as bad—she teaches history, so I had to listen to her talk all about U.S. involvement in the Middle East and the corruption of the military and how the war was a travesty and I was an obvious dupe, and on and on."

"What about your dad?"

"Don't remind me—he squandered the money my grandmother set aside for college for me and my brother. Then he had the nerve to be upset when I enlisted. No one in our family's ever been in the service, except for an uncle who went to Italy during World War II. That I would actually enlist, of my own free will, wasn't even believable to my family."

Ernesto shook his head. "Man, that's a mess. It's an honor in my family. They were thrilled—I'm the first one, too, but that's because I'm the first generation who's been a citizen."

Ernesto lit another cigarette. Charlie looked out at the horizon—mountainous terrain as far as he could see. "My brother was the worst," he said softly.

"Really?" Ernesto said.

Charlie nodded his head. "I never realized so many people were interested in my future."

"Yeah," Ernesto laughed and inhaled smoke, then let it out through his nose.

Jack fully entered Charlie's mind then, as he did several times a day. Charlie looked at his watch and translated the hour into California time, which he still thought of as the "real" time, as absurd as this was.

Where was Jack, and what was he doing now? It was painful not to know. It was 10 P.M. at home, which meant that he was probably off partying somewhere. It seemed to Charlie that Jack had been getting high and drinking even more than usual; if he talked to him after nine o'clock at night now, his speech was slurred and his reactions hyper. Charlie couldn't help worrying about him.

He'd woken up last night, his heart slamming in his chest, unable to remember where he was . . . then he heard Ernesto snoring beside him and slowly started to put the jigsaw puzzle together. But why did he feel so anxious? He thought of all the obvious hazards at hand—bombs and snipers—but that wasn't what was causing his panic. It was the thought of Jack, who he'd dreamed was sinking in a pit of quicksand, just like in the Tarzan movies they used to watch together as boys. Charlie was too far away to pull his brother out of whatever trouble he might get into—his deployment meant he'd had to let go of whatever rescue rope he'd used in the past.

Charlie's unit set up this outpost after climbing for hours, scrambling through creek beds and over crumbling rocks. By the time they'd arrived, Charlie had blood on his face from the thorn trees that snagged his skin as he blundered along. He'd been exhausted, but there was no one to complain to, nothing to be done. They were all in the same boat, laboring under heavy body armor, struggling to breathe in heat that would hit 120 by afternoon and only drop ten or so degrees at night.

And what were they doing exactly?

Looking for IEDs—according to Ernesto. What else? This seemed to be, more or less, his full-time job so far. The enemy had realized that full-out assaults were less effective than these deadly, nerve-racking explosions.

Charlie saw evidence of them everywhere—in the blackened metal piles that once were jeeps abandoned on the side of the road; in crippled villagers whose legs had been torn off, or their arms mangled.

In the first few months, he had already engaged in the most strenuous physical activities of his life—climbing mountains, walking in obscene heat, toting weight on his back like a burro. But what else physical had he ever done? Phys ed in high school? Handball at his gym?

Everything Jack had said about the service turned out to be true: Charlie wasn't cut out for the Marines or for desert life, though this was irrelevant now. He had signed up for the long haul. Except for going AWOL, which he would never do, there was no way out. He'd signed papers, as if in blood.

So far, this was the most dramatic instance of Charlie actively rebelling against his brother's opinion and venturing out completely on his own. Now he felt that he was paying for this folly daily.

He'd not only undergone a physical transformation but a mental one. He experienced fierce new emotions every hour that he spent here. Almost every minute, he was afraid—terrified, really—of some unseen danger or threat that it was hard to put his finger on but that followed him everywhere.

Life had become deadly serious. Each day, there were situations that required him to reach inside himself and come up with pockets of strength and fortitude that he'd never known he had.

He held an assault rifle to cover Ernesto while he went into a crumbling stone building that could be booby-trapped; he looked into the bloody face of an old woman who had gotten caught in the line of fire while she was standing in line to buy bread. He took into his arms a mongrel dog that had been hit by a military transport—a mutt with a slender snout and white spots reminiscent of their childhood dog, Joey. Could Charlie really pick him up, clean his wounds, and eventually bury him? Yes, yes, he could.

Dying wasn't an abstraction here but an every-day occurrence, as common as taking a breath. Any moment a sniper's bullet could travel through the air or an IED could explode, and you'd be gone, forever—all of you, every nickname and fondest dream, every fingerprint and strand of hair that had once been yours alone.

He tried not to show Jack how unnerved he felt when they talked on Skype. This usually was easy enough, particularly because the connection was so lousy; it was hard to see or speak to him in any extended, meaningful way. The service cut off or froze every few minutes.

Frankly, Jack seemed terrified about being so far away from him; Charlie could see it in his eyes and in the frequency of his calls. He had the impression that Jack would have preferred to keep Skype on indefinitely, just so he could experience some fragment of what his twin was enduring.

When it got too intense, Charlie fobbed him off on Ernesto, who found it easier to joke about the weather and the bad food. No one else called, because no one else knew how.

CHAPTER 5

That night Charlie fell asleep as soon as he got off patrol, only to be awakened what felt like minutes later. He'd been in the middle of a deep and complex dream when Ernesto shone a light in his eyes and shook him.

"Time to head out, dude."

Charlie rolled over with a groan, shielding his eyes. "What? You mean now?"

"Yeah, just got a call. Some big doings west of here—up and out."

"Aw, man." He rolled over, then sat up and rubbed his eyes. "What kind of doings?"

"Not sure—some kind of massacre in a village is what I hear."

"Great. What time is it anyway?"

"Four."

"Christ." He sat up for a moment, then stood and began reaching for his clothes.

Charlie looked over at Ernesto, who was standing there watching him.

"You ready to go?"

"I ain't going."

"Why not?"

"They need someone to stay here and monitor the computers and shit."

"Damn." Charlie didn't like going without Ernesto; somehow he considered him good luck.

"You'll be all right—be back before you know it."

Charlie was silent as he finished dressing.

They set out in a convoy in the fading darkness. In his Humvee were two blond, blue-eyed soldiers from the Midwest, Benjamin and Jim, and a young black guy from Brooklyn named JD. They all were laughing and smoking and drinking weak coffee with dried milk that someone had gotten at the last minute. Radio information kept filtering through. Ernesto was right: there'd been some kind of massacre.

They drove into the Afghan Valley, heading toward a village in the west. As the sun rose, terraced fields rose up before them. Charlie was only half awake, and he opened and closed his eyes at this dreamlike world—trees with gnarled apples on one side, a burned and twisted jeep on the margins of the road on the other. As they neared the village, the sun came up with a white ferocity, and a thin breeze blew a terrible scent their way.

"The village," Charlie said. "We must be almost there."

The platoon stopped, and they pulled up next to two other Humvees near an empty creek bed.

Oh, man, I don't want to go in there, Charlie thought just as Benjamin said to him, "Charlie, you and Jim check out the graveyard over there for weapons caches, and keep an eye on that ridge. We'll be back."

Benjamin and JD climbed out and joined other troops, who cautiously approached the mud and stone village. In the distance, a fruit orchard sat in a small fertile crescent. The rest was mountainous rock. Two mangy dogs barked and ran their way, and then a small herd of children appeared out on the bumpy dirt road, all chattering at once.

Even though heavy guns were mounted to their vehicles, the dusty-faced children ran right over to greet them.

"Sir, candy?" a small boy in a cap cried.

"I thought they were supposed to be frightened of us," Charlie said to Jim.

"Yeah." Jim handed the boy a couple pieces of Bazooka gum—the familiar wrapping looked surreal to Charlie in this new and foreign land. "They're scared of us, but they love us, too."

Charlie knew it was dangerous to let his guard down, but the kids were so adorable. He hoisted up a little girl with a shattered hand and carried her around on his shoulders for a few minutes before Jim gave him a warning look.

"You have dollar?" the girl asked, and he put her down abruptly. She was older than he thought—maybe as old as ten.

"Ask her if the Taliban's been here in the last days and if they harass them," Jim said to him.

"No, they not here," she answered without waiting for Charlie's question. She took the quarter he handed her as if it were solid gold. "Thank you," she said and ran off.

"She's probably lying," Jim said, giving him a rueful look as they watched the soles of her dirty feet recede into the distance.

The two soldiers walked through creek beds to a cemetery, where they found nothing but rock and thorny brush, not a weapon in sight.

All the while, Charlie kept studying the ridge that surrounded them. At one point he saw what looked like an auburn dog—perhaps a coyote—but the next second, it was gone.

They trudged back to the Humvee, over a punishing terrain of rocks and boulders. There was a buzzing menace in the air that Charlie could not ignore nor easily identify.

His feet hurt, he was starving, but even worse, he suddenly missed Jack with a ravening pain that took his breath away. *Where are you, brother? How did we ever allow ourselves to get so far apart?*

That morning, Charlie had heard Skype ring on his computer as he was getting ready to leave and get into the Humvee, but he ignored it—even though there was a chance it could be Jack. Charlie was trying to concentrate on the task at hand and didn't want to be distracted by his brother, whose anxiety was often infectious. He found it disorienting to talk to Jack, then walk a few yards and find himself in the heart of the hostile desert again. He also found it hard to talk about anything neutral or upbeat. He couldn't tell his brother what he was doing or even where he was doing it. Because of this, their conversations were often stilted and one-sided. Jack delivered news about their mutual friends—who'd lost a job or had broken up with a girlfriend. Or he talked about himself: he'd seen a movie or lost a filling; his car needed a new transmission.

Charlie often had trouble concentrating on all the facts and details, let alone even hearing them over the static. Sometimes he became exasperated with Jack's petty problems. *Who gives a shit about your transmission?* he wanted to say. *Do you realize where I am?* The people he once knew didn't even seem real to him in this world of sun and dust.

And he could never explain, even to Jack, how different it was here. Basic services that they had always taken for granted—hot showers, for example—were now luxuries. In the desert, water was liquid gold. The weather was no minor matter either; it was central to the day's mission and outcome. And the members of his team had become more than minor sidekicks and partners—they were blood brothers, who could, and often did, save your life.

Young men like JD, who'd put himself on the line for his unit and Charlie so many times that he'd lost count, or Joe, the farmer's son from Alabama, who was as right-wing as Charlie was liberal, yet told him after a recent firefight, "I love you, man—I really love you. We almost died together."

This was the kind of bond that Jack would miss out on entirely. Not only that, but he would be fiercely jealous if he knew how close Charlie had grown to these other men.

As often as Charlie wished that he had never come, he also wished that Jack could have accompanied him. As it was, there would always be a central event that he could never share with his twin—maybe the crucial event of his life. He felt guilty about this, as if Jack were being cheated, instead of him.

CHAPTER 6

It took more than half an hour for the traffic caused by the accident to clear so that Jack could finally move again. He couldn't stand to think of all the time he'd lost—more than 40 minutes. He shook himself alert and began driving again through the late-night streets. Traffic was sparse now, except for a few taxis. He had his laptop open on the passenger seat and reached over to click the wireless icon; the computer searched for a signal as he drove. He moved into the right lane and slowed down in front of various establishments, hoping to pirate an open-access Wi-Fi network.

Jenny's Cafe on the corner of Main and Summit had a network, but it was password-protected, as was the Creamery Ice Cream Shoppe and the Dixie Coffee Spot. He tried the hardware store, two insurance companies, and even a funeral home. All were locked.

Jack quietly cursed and pressed down the gas to leave downtown. Desperate for a connection, he decided to steer his car through a series of residential areas. He drove farther afield, out of the city center. His car, nearly alone on the sleepy, rain-soaked streets, emitted an otherworldly glow.

Various networks popped up on his laptop. Most were simply last names: the Sandy family, the Conners, Le Compte. All were locked. They appeared and disappeared in seconds. Then a new unlocked network appeared: the Tankian family. The signal was strong.

"Yes!" Jack said and pulled over to the curb.

Opening a browser, he sent Charlie an e-mail, typing like a machine gun.

are you ok? i need 2 talk to u!!

He hit SEND.

But even this didn't seem enough.

Next he opened a Skype window; he and Charlie had talked on Skype numerous times since he'd enlisted. Jack still couldn't get over the power of seeing his brother's living, breathing face, talking and laughing in real time, on another continent, with the sound of mortar exploding behind him.

Once he'd asked Charlie just to leave Skype on, even if he couldn't stay on it himself, and for an hour or so, Jack sat listening to the sounds of a marine's life halfway around the world. It sounded completely different from his California existence.

There were coughs and laughs and snippets of unintelligible conversation. There was an alarm, then a distant explosion; there was the beeping of Skype alerts and cell phone rings. He found it all fascinating—listening in to the most exotic and distant locale—a place where his brother was bound to remain without him.

On Skype tonight, Charlie's name was grayed out; he wasn't online. Jack smacked his hand against the steering wheel. He scrolled through other names on the Skype list, and found Ernesto Olveiros, one of Charlie's closest friends. Jack and Ernesto had talked several times before when he couldn't get ahold of Charlie. He was frequently on Skype, trying to call his family in Missouri. Besides that, he was friendly and eager to talk to Jack about Charlie—or anything else.

Jack was glad to find anyone who was in close proximity to his brother.

He clicked on Ernesto's name, and in a moment, his face appeared on the screen. The connection wasn't great; the image kept freezing, but Jack was still thrilled.

"Hey, hippie. How's slacker-ass commie life treating you?" Ernesto wore desert fatigues, a T-shirt, and sunglasses pushed back on his head. Charlie had told him that Ernesto had his own family, with two small kids, but he looked like a kid himself to Jack.

"Where's Charlie?"

"Made any hemp blankets lately?"

Gregg Braden & Lynn Lauber

"C'mon, man, where is he? Where are you guys?"

"I can't tell you that, dude. You know that."

The connection suddenly dropped. Ernesto's face froze.

The rain pounded against the hood of the car. The Wi-Fi bars indicated a weak signal, and Jack tried holding the laptop up in the air toward the house. The connection became only a little stronger. Jack quickly slapped the car into gear and coasted forward a bit, to get more in line with the house.

"Ernesto? Can you hear me?"

Ernesto's face became unfrozen, and Jack barely heard him say, "I can't hear you. It's not a very . . ." He faded out again.

"Is Charlie there? Is he okay?"

"He's fine . . . call back."

The words and images were skipping, then settling.

"Are you guys still in Kandahar? Is his unit out on a mission right now?"

Ernesto shifted uncomfortably. "Yes. See, I shouldn't have even told you that. What's with the third degree, dog?"

"Ernesto, please, it's important."

"Well, he's not anywhere where he can have a conversation right now. But they gotta be back by 1500 hours, 2:30 A.M. on your side. If you wanna wait up—"

"Tell him to Skype me the second he's back, okay? I'm going to try to stay online."

"Can't hear you."

"Tell him to call me!" Jack rubbed his temple.

"What's up with you, man?"

Even across the world, it must have been apparent that he was overwrought.

"I'm going to try to wait online, all right? I'll try to stay on Skype until he's back."

Ernesto leaned closer to the camera. "You in a car?"

Jack ignored the question. "If he gets back sooner, make sure he talks to me."

Ernesto's words and image skipped, then settled.

Jack put his hand to his head; something was happening again. He looked up at the rearview mirror into his own eyes. They glowed, and a strange halo of sparkling lights appeared around his head. Like hundreds of dancing stars, they grew steadily brighter.

He had a vision of a desert as seen out of a cracked window, sunglasses reflecting the sun.

"Hey?" Ernesto asked. "What's the matter with you? Are you okay, kid?"

Jack opened his eyes and blinked several times. Seeing Ernesto's face, he was about to respond when there was a banging sound from right next to him.

A gloved hand was knocking on the car window. Jack jerked around in panic to find a young security guard in a bulky uniform standing at the window, pointing his flashlight on him.

Glancing back in the rearview mirror again, Jack now saw that a security car had pulled up behind him. He realized that the headlights hitting the raindrops on his windows was probably the cause of the dancing lights.

"Shit," Jack muttered under his breath.

"Excuse me, sir?" The security guard's voice was so high that he sounded like an adolescent.

He tapped the window again, and Jack rolled it all the way down, unable to keep the annoyance from his voice.

"Can you please stop shining that light in my eyes?"

On the computer screen, Ernesto moved, leaning close to the camera.

"Jack? Are you there?"

"Hold on, Ernesto—"

The guard eyed the laptop suspiciously.

"Sir, what business do you have in this neighborhood?"

"I'm parked on a public street. *That's* my business."

"May I see your license and registration?"

"Hey, you're a security guard, not a cop. And I'm allowed to be here."

Jack turned back to Ernesto.

"Ernesto, don't hang up. Sorry—"

The guard pulled out his radio, and after a few bumbling seconds, announced in an officious voice, "I've got a 251 in progress at 1501 Euclid. Requesting police backup."

"What the hell is a 251?"

"Sir, you appear to be stealing Internet access."

Jack started to get out of the car, but the guy was so jumpy, he suddenly changed his mind. "You can't steal Internet access! It's in the air. It's not like stealing a car!"

"It's *exactly* like stealing a car."

Suddenly from the laptop, there was what sounded like a radio transmission of men yelling and swearing, and a far-off explosion.

Jack turned back to it. On the screen, Ernesto looked behind him, then turned back to the camera.

"Jack, I gotta go."

"Wait! What's happening? Ernesto!"

"Gotta go, dude."

"Tell Charlie—I'll be online no matter what," Jack said frantically. "I'll find a place."

But Ernesto was gone, and the Skype window went blank.

Jack was swept with an anxiety so strong that he knew he couldn't sit still, not for another moment.

"Sir, may I please see your identification—hey!"

The security guard stepped back just as Jack slammed the car into gear and peeled off. In the rearview mirror, he could see the guy fumbling with his cell phone.

Jack sped back into a commercial area where businesses were closed and dark.

"Where can I go? Where can I go?" he chanted out loud. Suddenly, he realized where he was. He turned the car around, and in a short time, pulled up in front of his high school.

He turned off his headlights and grabbed his laptop, clicking on the networks icon. The Roosevelt High network was unlocked.

"Yes!" Jack said. He clicked again, but found the connection was weak.

He looked around to see if there was somewhere he could park closer to the school buildings, but there were no other spaces. He slipped his laptop into his messenger bag, got out of the car, and began to climb through the bushes down to the school.

When he reached the fence, he slipped through a small break that looked as if it had been there for years.

Lights burned on the first floor of building one—the science department. One of the brightest areas was Peter Keller's physics classroom, where he'd created his own private world, suffused by the scent of cigarette smoke and fragrant coffee that he was bringing to a boil in a lab beaker. There he was, surrounded by books, cups, and food wrappers, with classical music—a cassette labeled "Research Mix 45"—playing in the background.

Peter lit a cigarette from the Bunsen burner and carefully placed it in a petri dish, his makeshift ashtray, then mixed the dark coffee with a bit of milk foam he procured from a silver cup and made himself a cappuccino. He removed a yellow disk of sugar cookie from a scale, pulled out a precision knife, and cut it into perfect quarters. All his actions were measured and exact, as if they were part of some solemn and solitary ritual.

Peter rented a small apartment on the other side of town, but he was rarely there; no one realized how many hours he spent in this classroom, his after-hours sanctuary. No one realized what a loner he'd become.

He ate a quarter of the cookie, then rearranged himself on his meditation pillow and closed his eyes.

When he opened them again, he stared transfixed at the chalkboard in front of him before he picked up a small tape recorder and began speaking. "Pull up the Michelson-Morley experiment for review. Cross-reference the Schrödinger equation with the Pribram/Bohm holonomic model. Also pull up any additional journal reports on the Geneva twin-photon experiment." He paused for a second. "If possible, find parallel examples dealing with quantum entanglement." His thoughts were interrupted by the sound of metal clinking. Outside, he could see the chain-link fence shaking in the wind.

The glow of the laptop screen illuminated Jack's face as he stood in the gravel driveway of the school's loading dock. The Skype window was open, but both Charlie's and Ernesto's names were inactive.

Suddenly a message appeared on the computer screen with a beep: low battery.

Jack whispered, "You've got to be kidding."

He snapped the laptop closed and studied the school building. Then he moved to the lit windows and started testing them to see if any were open.

Peter stood at the blackboard, a cigarette dangling from his lips as loud rock music blared from his stereo. He stood, jotting notes in chalk, absorbed in writing a complicated mathematical equation. He'd paused to consider what he had just written when he suddenly heard a thud out in the hall.

His face went pale as he turned and looked toward the door. He heard it again, louder this time. Someone was definitely there. He glanced at his watch, confused.

He moved over to extinguish his cigarette in the sink, waving his hands to disperse the smoke. Then he lowered the volume of the stereo; the room was silent for a moment. There was more noise, followed by a light tapping sound.

Peter picked up a mop from the corner, took a deep breath, and moved out into the hallway.

Jack had wedged open an upper window transom enough to reach in with his arm. Using a stick he tapped the lock of the window below, trying to release it. It worked. He pushed open the window, grabbed his messenger bag, and began to climb in.

At the same moment, Peter peered around the corner, at the end of the long hallway, holding the mop like a weapon.

"Hey!" he called.

The sound of Peter's voice took Jack by surprise, and he fell into the building with a thud, landing awkwardly on his left leg.

"Hey!" Peter yelled again. "What are you doing?"

Jack said, "I'm sorry. It's okay. I'm just trying to—"

"This is school property!" Peter said. "You're not supposed to be here."

Jack rubbed his ankle, wincing in pain. "Look, I know it's school property."

"You're breaking and entering!"

"I think I just broke my ankle." Jack started to stand up.

"Don't move! I'm calling the police right now."

"Why? Don't—please. I can explain."

Peter felt in his pocket for his phone, then realized that he'd left it back in his classroom. All the while, he continued staring at Jack. There was something vaguely familiar about him. "Just stay where you are. I'm going to get my phone and then I'm calling the police—"

"Hold on! I'm not trying to do anything bad. I just need to plug in my computer, okay?"

Jack started hobbling down the hall toward Peter.

"Don't come any closer. Do you have a gun?"

"It's just my computer," Jack said. "I'm not going to hurt you. I'm *not* trying to steal anything. I told you, I just need to plug in my computer."

"You broke in to plug in a computer?"

Jack was growing exasperated by so many questions; time was ticking away, and he couldn't seem to get his old physics teacher to understand his plight.

"Look, I tried to log on to the network from outside, but the signal was too weak. So then I made it through the fence to connect in the breezeway, and my battery started to die. Please, Mr. Keller, it's an emergency. I *have* to get online."

Peter stepped forward to see better, and something in his face relaxed.

"You're Charlie Franklin."

"Close. Jack. We're—"

"Twins," Peter said. "I remember now."

"Good memory."

"Class of 2005. Good students. What happened? You look like a hoodlum now."

"Why? Because I'm wearing a hoodie?" He slipped it off, revealing his long hair.

"No, because you're breaking into the school in the middle of the night." Peter stared at him for a moment. "Are you high?"

"Mr. Keller . . . look, my brother, he's a soldier in Afghanistan, and something's happening, okay? I have to reach him, right away. I have to get on Skype so I can talk to him. Please."

The plaintiveness in Jack's voice made a dent in Peter's doubts. *Why am I being so suspicious, anyhow?* he asked himself.

He gazed at his former student's face. He remembered him now perfectly, and his brother, too—intense young men with level hazel eyes who seemed so linked that it had been a little odd to encounter them as a pair. *How do you distinguish yourself when there is another one of you, so alike, so attuned?* he remembered wondering.

Like so many of his students, Charlie and Jack seemed on the brink of some critical turning point in their lives. And perhaps this had been it—one of them at war, the other at home.

Peter sighed. He hoped he wasn't making some grave error.

"Okay," he said to Jack. "Come on."

CHAPTER 7

Peter and Jack walked through the high school halls together, Jack limping heavily on his injured ankle.

"We'll get you some ice," Peter said, suddenly solicitous. "Do you think your ankle's really broken?"

"I don't know. Maybe I just twisted it."

They walked through the lobby, past the glass display of student photos. Peter glanced at Jack's photo, but actually stopped and stared at Charlie's—the same open sensitive face, but with close cropped hair and a more focused, intense look in his eyes.

"There he is," Jack said. "I can't believe he's so far away."

After a moment, he moved on and Peter followed.

"What are you doing here this time of night, anyway?" Jack asked him.

"Just grading . . . things," Peter mumbled. When they reached the physics classroom, Peter said, "Wait a minute," and went in alone.

He quickly tossed his cigarettes and ashtray into his desk, then pulled down the projection screen in front of the chalkboard so it covered his elaborate equation. Finally he opened the door for Jack.

"All right, come on. Try plugging in over there. In the third station, there's an outlet on the side."

In minutes, Jack's laptop was plugged in and set up at one of the student lab tables. He logged back on to Skype, but Charlie's name was still grayed out.

"Any word?" Peter asked.

Jack shook his head. "Nothing yet. Ernesto, a guy in his unit, said he's due back at the base by 2:30, our time."

Peter looked up at the clock—it was 1:34.

"Well, I'm sure he'll call. Can I get you anything? I just made some coffee."

"I don't do caffeine. You got any herbal tea?"

"You don't do caffeine? You've never had *my* coffee," Peter said proudly. He waited a moment. "You want herbal tea? All right. I think there's some in the teachers' lounge."

"Nah—that's all right. Maybe water?"

Peter filled a glass and handed it to him. "How long has your brother been in Afghanistan?"

"Two years. He should have been back by now, but you know how they extend everybody."

"Yeah. It must be hard. Him being so far away."

"Yeah." Jack rubbed his eyes. "Man, I'm getting crazy with this shit."

Peter stood beside him expectantly, waiting for more.

"This is the longest we've ever been apart. Plus, it's the first time we ever disagreed about anything as big as this."

"What did you disagree about?"

"Our father ended up spending our college nest egg, so we both knew we had to get to college on our own. Charlie became friendly with this recruiter who was hanging around town and decided to enlist. The recruiter tried to get me to enlist, too."

"And I take it you weren't interested?"

Jack gave him an incredulous look. "Are you kidding?"

"So what's your financial plan?"

"Computer work, teacher-assistant work—anything except the military. Anyway, when we were alone, I gave Charlie a hard time. He was always against war—both of us are. He's a vegetarian and pacifist, like me. But he wouldn't listen. He figured this was his ticket out, that his service would be short and that he'd collect a lot of money. We fought over it."

"A physical fight?"

"No, but yelling—and we never fight. I can count the times on one hand. So it was super upsetting. Before I knew it, I heard he was wearing his uniform around, and people were talking about how brave he was. God, it was like World War II or something."

"Maybe you were jealous?"

He shrugged. "Maybe. Problem is, we never got to really talk to each other alone after that discussion, everything happened so fast. I had to go out of town for a job, and when I came back, he was gone. Now it's almost impossible to get ahold of him for more than a few minutes . . . or make him understand what I'm saying."

"So exactly what happened to Charlie that you're so upset about now?" Peter asked him.

"I'm not totally sure," Charlie said. "But it could be really bad."

"What does that mean? Did you get a call? Was there something on the news?"

"No, no."

"Did this Ernesto guy tell you something?"

"Not really."

"I don't understand."

"Look, I don't know how to explain it, but I just know he's in serious danger right now."

"What do you mean, you just know?"

Jack took a deep breath. "I saw something happen to him."

"You *saw*?"

"Yes. Saw. A premonition, or a dream."

"Okay, so you broke into school in the middle of the night because you had a bad dream."

"My brother could be dying over there, and you're grilling me over using the school's Internet?"

"I'm grilling you about breaking into the school and then not being straight with me about why."

"But I am being straight with you—I *told* you I know something is wrong. I know something bad is going to happen to Charlie, unless I can warn him!"

"You don't *know* that."

"I do!"

"No, you *think* you do, but you don't have any factual information."

"Look, I don't expect someone like you to understand. I'm not making this up. We're *twins!* We just know things."

This stopped Peter, who looked at Jack's face, then turned and moved over to his desk.

Jack went back to his computer. Peter opened a book and pretended to read. Finally Jack looked up at Peter.

"You want facts? Okay! Jack and I were seven. We were at camp, playing by a river. I slipped on the mud. It was raining. The river was moving fast, and I fell into it. It was so cold that I could barely breathe. All I could do was try to keep my head above water. Charlie ran to get help from the counselor, and he told him what happened and that I was under an old bridge.

"I *was* under a bridge, but miles downstream from where we'd been playing. I was washed underneath this thing, and I grabbed on to a strut, and I was holding on for dear life. Charlie had no way of knowing that. Yet he knew. He knew exactly where I was. He *knew*." Jack paused and looked at Peter, who was listening to him closely. "I get it. You're a science teacher, and you don't believe in anything you can't prove with a stupid equation—"

"You have no idea what I believe."

"Whatever . . ."

There was a long silence between them; finally Peter spoke. "Look, I completely appreciate your concern for your brother, I do. I guess all I'm saying is that when you're upset, it's very easy to start using your imagination. And one can never over-estimate the power of a negative imagination."

Jack jumped to his feet and said fiercely, "It's not my imagination! I saw it through my heart. I *felt* it." He smacked his chest for emphasis. "It's here."

Peter stared at him, now more curious than skeptical. Something Jack said had struck a nerve. "What do you mean, you *felt* it?"

"It's beyond words, but it's real. Hasn't there ever been anything you just knew was true?"

Peter looked down at his messy desk, considering Jack's words. His eyes fell on a photo of Manuela.

"Look, I need to speak to my brother, Mr. Keller." He began making gathering movements, as if he were leaving. "I'll do it somewhere else if I have to—"

"All right, calm down," Peter said. "You can stay. Just promise me that when your brother calls and says he's fine, which he will, you'll go home and get some rest."

"Okay. Fair enough." Jack sat down at his laptop, while Peter picked up a notebook.

"Um, Mr. Keller?" Jack said a few minutes later.

Peter looked up at Jack, who was squirming in his seat. Unconsciously, he'd raised his hand just like a student.

"Yes?"

"I need to use the bathroom."

"You don't need permission. How old are you?"

"Can I trust you to keep an eye on the computer?"

Peter smiled in spite of himself. "Sure. Of course I'll keep an eye out for you."

As soon as he was alone, Peter let out a deep sigh, then went over and checked Jack's computer.

Nothing new. He returned to his desk, sipped his coffee, and stared at the sugar cookie on the plate. Two halves facing one another. He had a sudden realization. He dug in his pocket and pulled out a small tape recorder, hit rewind then listened to his own voice: "Pull up any additional journal reports on the Geneva twin-photon experiment. If possible, find parallel examples dealing with quantum entanglement."

Peter raised the projection screen and began writing on the chalkboard. He stopped the recorder as Jack reentered. Jack hesitated when he saw that the screen was raised, exposing a massive equation on the chalkboard.

Around the equation were all sorts of other equations, lists, and names. By now Peter was writing something near the top of the board.

"Man, what is *that*? I hope that's not what you're giving for homework these days."

Peter turned around, pulling down the screen to cover what he had been writing.

"No, this is my personal madness . . . my private research."

"So why do you keep it hidden? Is it some kind of secret?"

"No, I've just learned over the years that it's good to be cautious with whom I share my ideas."

"So can I see it?"

Peter hesitated, then raised the screen again "Okay, knock yourself out. Just don't go telling any of your hoodlum friends about it."

Jack approached the board and studied it.

"Did you end up going to college?" Peter asked.

"Art school."

Jack read the top line above the equations out loud. "The Divine Matrix: An Ancient Approach to a Unified Field Theory, by Dr. Peter Keller."

"That's just a working title. It's kind of been co-opted by the popular culture. But it's still better than a lot of them out there."

Jack examined a list of names on the side chalkboard: "Supersymmetry, the Higgs Field, the unified field."

"Those are all related terms," Peter said.

Jack continued reading: "Blueprint, grid, virtual fluctuation field, ether."

"Yeah, those have a little too much baggage. Bad associations."

"Quantum noise, quantum soup, blanket, the Force, Brahman, the net of Indra, the mind of the universe, the web of Spider Grandmother."

"That's a Hopi story."

"Yeah, I know. My roommate's all into the Native American stuff." Jack stared at the list of names, then pointed at the equations. "But how does *this* relate to all of *this?*"

Peter drew a circle on the board and cut it into quarters. "All over the world, we have different languages, all basically describing the same thing." He stopped drawing and stared at the circle for a moment.

"Would you like a cookie?" Peter asked. This seemed out of the blue, and Jack was perplexed but said okay. Peter walked over to his desk, returned with the plate, and continued.

"All these different cultures, all describing the same thing, which is the fabric of the universe or 'the mind of God'—if you believe in that sort of thing."

Jack looked at him in surprise. "Me? How about you? A scientist using the *G* word? Isn't that heresy?"

"Well, there are separate camps. You have the religious community, who believe in the existence of God without actual proof. And you have the scientific community who are equally committed to the Big Bang theory, which also, by the way, lacks verifiable evidence."

"Right, the whole Creationists versus the old Darwinians thing."

"Correct. Which brings to mind my favorite adage, *All truths are but half truths.*"

"The law of polarity," Jack said, picking up a cookie.

Peter looked at Jack, impressed. "Listen to you—yes, the law of polarity."

"We *do* read books in art school," Jack said.

"Then you know that any universe that is composed of inextricably linked pairs of opposites, like light and dark, hot and cold, up and down, life and death . . . that it's very easy to become overwhelmed by the apparent contradiction inherent in all things. Right? So? We have these buffers that come up, that act as blinders to keep us from going crazy in the face of all this conflicting information. But, and here's another contradiction, the same blinders that keep us from losing our minds are the ones that keep us in the dark, by not letting us see the whole picture of the paradoxical nature of things."

"Well, I understand that, but it's this math stuff that's beyond me."

Peter smiled. "I think you might understand that better than I do."

"What's that supposed to mean?"

Peter went to his desk and took out his cigarettes and ashtray.

"That means if you ever tell anyone I was smoking in here, I'll kill you."

He lit up, then pushed open a classroom window, and leaned on the sill. Smoke from his cigarette spilled out into the night.

Jack said, "What's with these persistent rumors about your being a government man, working for NASA?"

Peter laughed. "Why is it that every scientist is supposed to have worked at NASA? No, I was at a place called Fermilab, outside of Chicago. At the time, it housed the world's largest particle accelerator."

"Particle accelerator? What's that do? Speed up particles?"

"You're familiar with the Hubble Telescope?"

"Yeah."

"Well, Hubble is a giant telescope that allows you to see into the farthest reaches of outer space. The particle accelerator is a giant microscope that allows you to view the farthest reaches of *inner* space."

"So what do you see?"

"Heavenly bodies of subatomic particles. The Higgs boson, the holy grail of modern physics, connected to the Higgs field."

"Yeah, those are just words to me." Jack pointed at the board. "What does the Higgs field mean?"

"Well, one of the roles of science is to create an accurate understanding of the universe. The current model, the so-called Standard Model, is incomplete. It's like a puzzle that's missing some very important pieces. Such as, why does mass exist? And proving the existence of this all-pervasive field of energy—Higgs field—it would be the key to pulling a lot of these missing pieces together."

"Okay, I get it. Wow. So, you were like the real deal."

"I got a little attention coming out of grad school—"

"Where?"

"A place back East . . . MIT."

"Dude, I've heard of MIT," Jack said, rolling his eyes.

"Right. So, yeah, it was a heady thing, being anointed and admitted into that particular inner sanctum. Every science major's dream come true, getting to plumb the depths of life on Earth and beyond, to be on the forefront of solving the great enigmas of how the universe came into existence.

"It all felt very important down there with the subatomic particles." Peter put out his cigarette. His face had paled, and his words grew halting. "Then one day they got ahold of me at work because I hadn't been back to my apartment for three days. They were calling to tell me that my girlfriend, ugh . . . such a deeply inadequate term to describe what she was . . . the love of my life,

Manuela, had been found dead. Hit and run. She was on a bicycle one minute and gone the next."

Peter pointed to her photo on his desk.

"Wow, that's heavy," Jack said, looking at the photo for the first time. The woman staring out at him had a sensitive yet serious face. She wasn't smiling, but looking intently at the camera, as if in challenge. "I'm really sorry."

"I kinda cracked up, or cracked open for a little bit. Lost it for a while there. The shock of it sent me on a search, which funnily enough, took me all the way back around to something that had been there all along."

"What was that?"

Peter got up and moved toward the front of the room.

"There's a quote, by one of my heroes, Max Planck, godfather of quantum physics: 'All matter exists by virtue of a force . . . and we must assume that behind that force . . . is the existence of a conscious and intelligent mind. The Matrix of All Matter.' And suddenly I saw what all the equations and theories had been leaving out. *Consciousness*."

Outside there were thunder and lightning.

Peter smiled at Jack. "Looks like the universe agrees."

"Let's take a walk," Jack said. "I need to clear my head."

"Good idea. The teachers' lounge should be open."

CHAPTER 8

Peter and Jack walked down the dark hallway; both were deep in thought.

Eventually Jack said, "You know what I remember from your class? That story about the plate glass. Who was that? Einstein?"

"It was actually his colleague John Wheeler."

"Yeah. Something about how scientists are always viewing the universe safely behind a thick slab of plate glass. It's all happening out there somewhere. Separate from us."

They turned a corner and headed down the stairs.

Peter said, "But we now know, that's just not how things work. To observe an object as small as an electron is to *change* the object. And beyond that, more recently, we've found that at even deeper quantum levels, to observe something is to actually *create* it! If we really want to know the true nature of things, Wheeler suggested—"

Jack finished his thought, using a German accent, "Ve must smash the plate glass."

"He was American. But good accent. And yes— once we remove this artificial barrier, we can no longer deny that we are intrinsically linked to this outer space through our inner space consciousness. We are not observers, but participants."

The teachers' lounge held tables, a microwave, and a wall-length chalkboard. When they arrived, Peter asked Jack if he wanted something to drink.

Peter began to dig through boxes of tea.

"The herbal stash. Pomegranate. Mellow Mint. Peach Orchard. How about Lemon Zinger?"

"Fine. Zinger's good."

Peter smelled the bag. "Really? You want something with it?"

"No, I'll take it straight."

Peter made the tea, then poured out a bowl of mixed nuts. They sat together at one of the tables.

"So, then what's the big difference between what you're doing, and the Standard Model with the Higgs thing?" Jack asked.

"Well, for starters, my math is a lot prettier. But beyond that, there are implications, which is what really matters. What are the implications of this field of subtle energy, in which all things live and breathe and have their being? The idea at the core of it is the oldest idea in the books. We are one. The uni-verse. The poetry of oneness.

"We're not separate objects floating around in empty space, but part of one undulating, pulsing, multidimensional uni-being organism, from the realm of all suns and planets down to the subatomic quantum level. All vibrating together at varying frequencies, transmitting, absorbing, digesting, reflecting, radiating light and energy, endlessly held together by this invisible yet omnipresent force of consciousness."

Jack's eyes were alight with amazement as he listened to Peter, whose own face was flushed.

"Dude, you need to go to Burning Man, because they would friggin' love you there."

The two men watched it rain for a moment. Then Jack said, "So before, what was that thing you started to show me—when you were drawing the circle?"

Peter crossed to the back wall, picked up a piece of chalk and drew a wheel. "Actually, this was told to me by my mother when I was a kid." He started drawing spokes. "All paths and religions are like spokes on a wheel. And the farther out you are from any of them, the more superficial, the more disparate and distant, they'll seem from one another. However, the deeper you go, the more similar they become. They meet in the center.

"All things are interconnected through consciousness. From the farthest reaches of outer space, the macrocosm; to the farthest reaches of inner space, the microcosm and quantum physics—all are reflections of one thing. I had the audacity to put out a paper that intimated that science is just another teaching trying to find its way into the center of the circle. The aim of which is consciousness."

Jack said, "That must have gone over great with the scientific community."

Peter quickly erased the chalkboard in the lounge and smiled ruefully. "Yeah, it was a big hit. That's why I rarely publish anymore."

"To hell with them, dude. They're all just part of the system," Jack said. "So is that why you're hiding out here?"

Peter seemed startled by his comment; this conversation was getting too close for comfort. The truth was that he preferred the lab to his apartment, where everything reminded him of Manuela. It was easier here, where he could control his environment, just like one of his experiments. None of these were topics he intended to discuss with Jack—or anyone else.

"Who says I'm hiding out? I like to think I've chosen to cultivate my ideas in an open-minded atmosphere. There's something about being around kids. Especially when they're this age, at the dawn of self-awareness. They're so open, and they're asking questions. It's inspiring—they're not afraid to indulge in wild and outrageous possibilities."

"Is that why you said I understood your ideas better than you do?"

"Well, that's part of it. But it has to do with this." Peter touched his chest. "Direct apprehension. The power of the heart to transcend thought.

We're talking about the field of subtle energy that is the conduit between our consciousness and that of all worlds. It's in us. Small children have access to it. They don't separate themselves from their world. But as we grow older, buffers emerge. Societal indoctrinations start to hypnotize us, and gradually there's a tendency to lose that connection. Soon, *boom*, we're shut down, and it takes a shock to blow the heart back open to the intuitive, nonverbal language of feeling."

Jack nodded. "When you're a twin, you can never entirely separate yourself from the outside world. You look over there, and, well, *there you are*. Maybe that's why we still retain this sensation of just knowing through feeling."

There was a crack of thunder as the huge downpour increased outside, giant raindrops pelting down from the sky.

Peter studied Jack closely for a moment, then nodded. "Yeah, there may be something to that. Sympathetic resonance. There was this experiment in Geneva in 1997, where a scientist took a photon, a single particle of light, and split it into two separate twin particles with identical properties. Then they fired the twins in opposite directions down two fiber-optic pathways for a distance of seven miles, so by the time each twin reached its target, fourteen miles separated them. At that point they were forced to choose between two random routes that were identical in every respect.

"The two particles made exactly the same choice at exactly the same time. Each time the physicist repeated the experiment, the results were the same. Information was being passed between the two particles instantaneously. Somehow they were communicating. This phenomenon is referred to as quantum entanglement."

Jack said, "So it's almost going to a molecular level—Charlie and me—quantum entanglement."

"Or 'spooky action at a distance'—that's what Einstein called it. Could be a good title for my book," Peter said, taking a drag from his cigarette.

Jack said, "But wait a minute. If even science is saying we're psychically connected, then there really must be something wrong with Charlie."

"Science would never say 'psychically connected.' It's all just speculative . . . we're just talking."

"Yeah, we're talking *too* much. What time is it anyhow?"

Peter looked at his watch. His expression was enough; Jack took off running toward the physics lab.

Jack tore into the room and went straight to his laptop.

"Charlie! I'm sorry, I'm here, don't hang up!" He stopped dead in his tracks.

On the computer screen, Charlie's name was still grayed out. So was Ernesto's. No messages. Nothing.

Peter walked into the room. "Jack!"

Jack quickly checked his e-mail. Nothing. "Oh, God. No!"

"Did you miss him? What happened?"

"He didn't call. Something really *did* happen."

"Jack, calm down. Listen to me. You don't know for sure."

"Or what if he did call, and I missed it! Because we were so busy talking!" Jack began to pace back and forth, his fists clenched, a strange look on his face.

Peter studied him and made a decision. "What did you see, Jack? Tell me now. What did you see?"

"I saw Charlie in the desert. I saw sand and a hill and a ridge. And in the distance what looked like a coyote—"

"A coyote?"

"Or something like one . . . and the guys, they were talking. But then there was this horrible buzzing, screaming sound! And then, I felt it burning through me! This horrible feeling! Burning through me!"

Enraged, Jack pushed over a lab table, causing equipment to crash to the floor.

"Jack, that's not happening. Get it out of your head. That's not real."

"It was real. Why would I see it if it wasn't real?" Jack put his hands to his temples, his breathing strained.

"I don't know. Maybe it was a premonition like you said—"

"But how can I warn Charlie if I can't speak to him?"

"All right, just relax, Jack. It'll be okay."

Jack breathed deeply as he focused on a large poster of outer space that hung on the wall beyond Peter—a poster of endless stars.

After a moment, he closed his eyes, and before he knew it, he was envisioning another flash of bright sunlight and then a Humvee followed by two other army vehicles, moving across the desert. The caravan was heading in the opposite direction from the last time he'd pictured it.

Jack fell back against the wall and put his face in his hands. He was shaking.

"Oh, my God, it's happening, right now! I can feel it! Charlie . . ."

Peter went to Jack and grabbed him by the arms, trying to control him. Jack struggled but ended up falling to the floor. Peter got down by his side and tried to calm him.

"Jack, listen! Panic doesn't help. It's a waste of time. There's a link between you and your brother, so use it—like a radio frequency."

"I want him back," Jack wept.

"*Wanting* won't work. You have to focus."

"I don't know how! It's too late."

"It's *not*. Bring him into focus. Open your heart up to him. And make him aware that you're guiding him back to safety."

"I can't," Jack cried, sounding like a small boy. "I don't know how."

"What does it feel like to know he's safe? What would it feel like to look up at that screen and see your brother's face on it?"

Jack did his best to look up at the computer, tears welling in his eyes.

"It feels good. It makes me feel so relieved."

"What are you going to say to Charlie?"

"I don't know, I don't know. Charlie, please be okay."

"He *is* okay, Jack. He is! Now, let him know how important he is. Use the energy field that connects you to see that he's fine. What else are you going to say?"

Jack's face was transformed by hope. "Charlie, you jerk! I thought something happened to you, but you're okay, you're safe."

Jack closed his eyes. He could see inside the moving Humvee.

Charlie sat in the front seat, talking with the driver. Suddenly Charlie stopped and turned to look behind him, as if he'd heard someone's call. He shook his head, as if to dislodge the sound.

The driver asked, "What's wrong?"

"I don't know—I hear something. Do you?"

The driver looked at him skeptically. "Nah, man. I don't hear anything. Are you okay?"

Back in the physics room, Jack opened his eyes. He appeared to be in a completely altered state.

Peter leaned down to him and said, "Stay connected. Let Charlie know how important it is to you that he's safe. Show him how much you love him. Wake him up with that love to another level of feeling. And awareness. Of everything around him."

Jack shut his eyes again, and this time, he saw his brother even more clearly, bumping along in the Humvee, light glinting off his sunglasses. He was still chatting with the other soldiers.

"Yes, Charlie's all right," Jack said. "I see him. He's safe."

The Humvee reached an area where there was a high hillside ridge, now on the right side of the caravan.

Tears poured down Jack's face. "He's smiling. He's alive."

There was a sudden flash. On the desert hill up ahead, an animal resembling a coyote stood on the ridge.

Jack gave an echoing cry, "Look up, Charlie!"

Charlie stopped talking and cocked his head, as if he'd heard something again.

An echo of Jack's shout traveled across space and time. *"Look up!"*

"Jack?" Charlie whispered, then turned in slow motion and looked up at the ridge.

Simultaneously, Jack opened his eyes, turned, and looked in the same direction as his brother.

Jack's eyes fluttered. Emotionally exhausted, he passed out.

Peter positioned him comfortably on the floor. He grabbed his meditation pillow from his desk and placed it under Jack's head.

"Jack, you're going to be okay. Everything's going to be okay," he whispered.

CHAPTER 9

The rain had stopped, and the clouds were gone, leaving the sky the tenderest shade of blue. The clock in the classroom read 6:15. Weak rays of morning sunlight slanted through the venetian blinds. Jack was curled up on the floor sleeping, Peter's jacket covering him.

Peter sat in front of Jack's computer, his head resting in his arms on the lab table, hovering in the region between sleep and wakefulness. Suddenly there was a *ding* sound, signifying an incoming e-mail.

The sound was loud enough to fully awaken Peter. He had been having a dream, and he sat for a moment to see whether he could recall it. The dream had been about Manuela, as so many of his dreams were. He almost always dreamed about her face, either flashing by in a passing car or standing at an apartment window—it was always fleeting, always heart tugging. But this dream had been the most powerful and bizarre. She had been flying through the air and had urged him to join her.

"Wait, you have to show me how," he'd cried out.

But she only laughed at this. "You *know how.* Come on!" And as he woke, he was doing it, soaring over a vast ocean with her shadow far ahead of him, into the blueness.

He took a moment to bring himself back to the lonely present, to the reality in which she was no longer alive. Then he stood and walked over to Jack's computer screen, where he found an e-mail from Ernesto Olveiros, with the subject line "Charlie." Rubbing his eyes, Peter headed over to wake Jack.

Yet when he reached him, he hesitated for a moment, then went back and opened the e-mail himself.

It read:

Buddy, something's wrong. Charlie's unit still hasn't come back yet, and they're way overdue. We haven't been able to make radio contact, but will keep you posted.

Peter whispered, "Oh, God."

Peter sat in a chair in the hallway, looking out the windows at the quiet school grounds outside.

At the far end of the hall, a janitor named Janice rounded the corner with her mop. Janice was in her 40s and had worked at the high school for almost as long as Peter had. She usually stopped to talk to him about her life, particularly since they tended to be the only ones at school on a Saturday, though today he was reluctant to engage her.

"Morning, Mr. Keller."

"Morning, Janice," he said in a voice that sounded subdued, even to him.

She gave him a second look, but plunged on anyhow. "How are the big ideas coming? You pull one of your all-nighters?"

Peter looked up at her with exhausted eyes and laughed ruefully. "You could say that."

"Looks like it was a rough one, eh?"

"Yeah, I think I might have made a few miscalculations last night," he said.

"Well, sorry to hear that," Janice said, as she started to mop the floor around him. "Maybe you should go outside and take a walk. Get out into nature for a while. That usually helps clear the mind."

Peter sat for a moment, looking at the floor, then up at her again. Janice had never said anything remotely like this to him in the past.

"Something wrong?"

He shook his head slightly. "No, no. Thanks, Janice. You're probably right."

When she was gone, he opened the door and stepped outside on the school lawn, where he usually went only to smoke a cigarette. In fact, he had one in his palm right now.

The air was fresh from the drenching rain and smelled sweet and clean. Peter put the cigarette back in the packet and took a deep breath instead. A plain brown bird on an overhead branch made a long trill, as if calling to him. He didn't know the name of the bird, but that a creature so small and drab could produce such an elaborate song made something stir inside him.

After a few moments, he walked inside the school. Back in the classroom, he stood over Jack, who was still lying on the floor, deeply sleeping.

"Jack? Jack, wake up."

Jack opened his eyes and sat up bolt upright to find Peter hovering in front of him.

"What's wrong?" he asked immediately.

Peter looked extremely uncomfortable.

"Listen, Jack. As much as I wanted this to work out, it wasn't my place—"

Jack interrupted, "What are you talking about?"

"It was wrong of me to have supported this idea." He hesitated and tried a new tack. "Look, we all want to believe in magic and miracles—"

"Mr. Keller—"

Peter plunged on. "But sometimes the truth can be hard to take." He hesitated again; every time he looked at Jack's face, he realized he was getting nowhere.

Jack said, "You know, I think you know a lot more about the heart than you give yourself credit for."

"Look, I'm trying to tell you I'm sorry. For everything. For turning your situation into some kind of experiment, for getting your hopes up—"

"He's okay. Charlie's okay," Jack said.

Peter studied Jack's face. He looked calm and self-assured.

"What?"

"He's okay."

Peter asked, "How do you—"

Jack smiled. "I just know."

Peter lowered his head; this made him feel even worse. "Oh, Jack. This is serious. There's something on your computer you should see."

"From Charlie?"

Peter took a deep breath. Just as he was about to answer, there was the bleeping sound from the computer, signaling a Skype caller invitation.

Jack jumped to his feet and ran to the computer. On the screen was a Skype name list, and Charlie's name had changed from gray to green, from passive to active. A dialogue box popped up on the screen: "Charlie would like to open a video discussion."

Jack looked over at Peter with a radiant smile.

"You had me going, Mr. Keller."

Peter looked over at him, utterly confused.

Jack hit the accept button. On the computer, Charlie's face appeared and smiled into the camera. Except for his mussed fatigues and closely shaved haircut, he looked exactly like Jack.

"What's up with you, bro?" he said. "Half of Afghanistan told me I had to call you as soon as I came in. What's the deal?"

Jack's smile was radiant. "Charlie, you ass, I thought something had happened to you! But you're safe. You're really okay?"

"Yeah, yeah. I'm okay."

Behind Jack, Peter put a hand over his heart.

"What happened?" Jack asked.

"Classified, bro."

"What's that mean?"

"Jack, classified means I can't tell you."

On the other side of the world, Ernesto stuck his head into the video window.

"Jack, get your brother to quit acting like a macho shithead and tell you what a hero he is." He playfully shook Charlie by the shoulders. "This dude's gonna get a freakin' medal."

"C'mon, man. Tell me! I was terrified. You have no idea what kind of night I've had," Jack said.

Charlie drank some water from a canteen and wiped his face with a handkerchief. He looked deeply into the Skype camera at his brother.

Then he said, "Okay, but this is just between us." He leaned closer and lowered his voice. "Early this morning we got sent out to check out this village that was supposedly ambushed. On the way, there's an area with hills on one side. I was assigned to check out the ridge line. And I saw a coyote standing up there, and suddenly I thought of you. I had this flash of that camp we use to always go to as kids, remember? Coyote Camp?"

"Coyote Valley Youth Camp, man," Jack said with a grin.

"Yeah! Thinking about it really made me miss my hippie brother."

Jack beamed and looked over at Peter with a knowing, affectionate smile.

Charlie continued, "We spent hours around that village, looking for armaments, checking out rumors of a massacre. And as we were heading back to base, we passed the ridge again where I'd seen the coyote, and then I heard you, bro. I really heard you, calling me, warning me. Suddenly I had this *feeling*. You know?"

Jack nodded, his eyes damp.

Charlie said, "And then it hit me. There *aren't* any coyotes in Afghanistan. So I stopped the whole caravan, and everybody started cussing me out. And then we spotted it, up on the ridge line. Right where I thought I had seen that coyote, we saw this dude running off. Turned out he'd just planted an IED. If we'd gone three hundred feet forward—well, let's just say it wouldn't have been pretty, man."

Jack took a deep breath, and he and Charlie sat for several minutes in silence, their heads bowed. To Peter, they almost looked as if they were praying.

Charlie was the one who eventually broke the spell. "So that's what happened. What's up with you, bro? Are you in some kind of laboratory or something?"

Jack didn't know what to say. He looked over at Peter, who nodded and said quietly, "We are."

"So what did you want to tell me about when you called? Was there something specific?"

Jack rubbed his face and looked at Peter. "Nothing specific, man, just this feeling. It's over now. I have them all the time about you."

Charlie laughed. "Yeah, I know. Me, too. Remember that time when Mom . . ."

Peter got up in the middle of what was turning out to be another story and left the brothers to reminisce as he walked outside to have a cigarette.

As he exited the building, he saw a line of bikers speeding by—the last was a woman with long black hair who raised her arm to wave as she disappeared around a corner. Peter was fairly sure that she was signaling to someone else nearby, but he chose not to look over his shoulder to verify this; for those few moments, he decided to be someone other than a scientist, to be a man receiving a final signal from his lover.

After he smoked his cigarette, he slipped quietly back into the classroom, where Jack and Charlie were still talking. He stopped at the pile of papers on his desk and began sorting them into two folders that had been impossible to see before—one marked "Current," the other, "To File."

Most were his own research papers, nearly ready for publication or review. All he had to do was retype them, stick them in envelopes, and mail them. He added Dori's manuscript, which he had ignored for so long, to the top of the "Current" file. And then he leafed through a pile of photos of Manuela, one after another, of her sitting in a café, smiling at him from various spots in his apartment, looking out at him with frank love across space and time.

Peter rearranged the stack and placed them in the "To File" folder, then shut it and turned to look at Jack, who was in the midst of retelling Charlie some childhood story that featured their grandmother. Peter, loath to interrupt, put the "Current" folder into his briefcase, slipped out into the hall, and quietly shut the door.

A quick calculation told him that Jack and Charlie were approximately 8,000 miles apart, but that didn't seem to make any difference. Just as his experiments had suggested so many years ago, they were still connected.

Outside, Peter turned into a northwesterly breeze as he dialed Dori's number on his cell phone. After a moment, an icon on his phone displayed two hands clasping together as the phone began to ring, and Peter waited for Dori to answer: *Connected*.

We all are, he thought, filling his lungs with the pure scent of April.

He was more sure of it now than ever.

ABOUT THE AUTHORS

Gregg Braden is a *New York Times* best-selling author, a former senior computer systems designer for Marietta Aerospace and computer geologist for Phillips Petroleum, and the first technical operations manager for Cisco Systems. For over 26 years he has searched the remote monasteries of Egypt, Peru, and Tibet for the life-giving secrets that were encoded in the language of our most cherished traditions. His work has led to such pioneering books as *The Divine Matrix, Fractal Time,* and *Deep Truth.* Gregg's work is published in 17 languages and 27 countries and shows beyond any reasonable doubt that the key to our future lies in the wisdom of our past.

Website: **www.greggbraden.com**

Lynn Lauber is a fiction and nonfiction author, teacher, and book collaborator. She has published three books of her own with W. W. Norton & Co., as well as many collaborations with other authors. Her specialties include fiction, personal narrative, and self-improvement. Her essays have appeared in *The New York Times.* She has abridged audio books for such authors as John Updike, Oliver Sacks, Oprah Winfrey, and Gore Vidal.

Website: **www.lynnlauber.com**

HAY HOUSE FILMS
Presents

The *Tales of Everyday Magic* Series
Buy the feature film *Entanglement* on DVD
Exclusively at **www.hayhouse.com**

Also Available

Painting the Future
DVD with Bonus Material • $14.95

Inspired by the writings of best-selling author Louise L. Hay, *Painting the Future* reveals how the thoughts we choose create the life we live.

On the second floor of a low-income apartment complex lives Jonathan Page. Once an established painter, Page now lives in complete darkness, rarely leaving his apartment and angry at the world. From the courtyard below, nine-year-old Lupe Saldana takes notice of Jonathan. Determined to save up for a dream quinceañera dress, Lupe extends herself as hired help for all the personal errands and daily chores that Jonathan can no longer do himself. Through this proposition, a friendship begins to blossom, and Lupe's optimistic innocence slowly breaks down the wall of Jonathan's guarded brokenness.

The Magic Hand of Chance
DVD with Bonus Material • $14.95

Based on the common underlying theme of the writings of Louise L. Hay and Dr. Wayne W. Dyer— the notion that if you change your thoughts, you can change your life—this film beautifully illustrates the magical power of belief.

Filmed in Vienna against the backdrop of a traveling Russian circus, *The Magic Hand of Chance* is the true story of a clumsy magician whose life is turned around when two clowns trick him into thinking he has received the highest honor by a magicians' society in America. Because he starts to *believe* he is great, he ultimately *becomes* great.

My Greatest Teacher
DVD with Bonus Material • $14.95

Based on the true life story of best-selling author Dr. Wayne W. Dyer, *My Greatest Teacher* is a compelling drama that explores the transformational power of *forgiveness*.

Dr. Ryan Kilgore is a college professor struggling to take his career to his desired level of success, while battling the very demons that are keeping him from achieving it. Kilgore is tormented by the memories of his father's abandonment, yet his wife and child are the ones who pay the price. Upon losing his grandmother, Kilgore desperately seeks the closure that he needed so long ago as he puts his future in jeopardy for a journey into the past. Through a series of mysterious and serendipitous events, a path opens that leads Kilgore to his father—and to making the choice to rebuild everything he has destroyed as a result of what had been destroying him.

Order Your Copies Today!
DVDs Available Exclusively at
www.hayhouse.com

VISIONS

Hay House, Inc., P.O. Box 5100, Carlsbad, CA 92018-5100
(760) 431-7695 or (800) 654-5126
(760) 431-6948 (fax) or (800) 650-5115 (fax)
www.hayhouse.com® • **www.hayfoundation.org**

We hope you enjoyed this Hay House book. Sign up for our
exclusive free e-newsletter featuring special offers, contests,
behind-the-scenes author interviews, movie trailers, and even
more bonus content, with the latest information on exciting
new Hay House products.

Sign Up Here www.hayhouse.com

Also Visit www.HealYourLife.com

The destination website for inspiration, affirmations, wisdom,
success, and abundance. Find exclusive book reviews,
captivating video clips, live streaming radio, and much more!

HEAL YOUR LIFE ♥   HAYHOUSE RADIO))

www.hayhouse.com®   www.healyourlife.com®   www.hayhouseradio.com®

Published and distributed in Australia by:
Hay House Australia Pty. Ltd., 18/36 Ralph St.,
Alexandria NSW 2015 • *Phone:* 612-9669-4299
Fax: 612-9669-4144 • www.hayhouse.com.au

Published and distributed in the United Kingdom by:
Hay House UK, Ltd., 292B Kensal Rd., London W10 5BE
Phone: 44-20-8962-1230 • *Fax:* 44-20-8962-1239
www.hayhouse.co.uk

Published and distributed in the Republic of South Africa
by: Hay House SA (Pty), Ltd., P.O. Box 990, Witkoppen 2068
Phone/Fax: 27-11-467-8904 • www.hayhouse.co.za

Published in India by: Hay House Publishers India,
Muskaan Complex, Plot No. 3, B-2, Vasant Kunj,
New Delhi 110 070 • *Phone:* 91-11-4176-1620 •
Fax: 91-11-4176-1630 • www.hayhouse.co.in

Distributed in Canada by: Raincoast,
9050 Shaughnessy St., Vancouver, B.C. V6P 6E5
Phone: (604) 323-7100 • *Fax:* (604) 323-2600
www.raincoast.com

Made in the USA
Lexington, KY
27 May 2012